CW00820024

Carol
MCALLISTER

THE GIRL THAT FELL
OUT OF
THE FAMILY TREE

novum pro

This book is also
available as
e-book.

www.novum-publishing.co.uk

© 2024 novum publishing

ISBN 978-3-99146-681-9
Editing: Atarah Yarach
Cover photo: Andrew7726,
Zdenek Sasek I Dreamstime.com
Cover design, layout & typesetting:
novum publishing

www.novum-publishing.co.uk

Print product with financial
climate contribution
ClimatePartner.com/16547-2311-1001

Contents

CHAPTER ONE

PART ONE:

NEVER WATCH YOUR PARENTS HAVING SEX

Lucinda Grey grew up feeling at odds with herself, her family and surroundings. Despite loving parents, it was clear to her from a young age that she simply didn't belong. One event, at the very heart of summer, shook her to the core, and made her question her very existence. Her primary teacher later revealed all, when she led the whole class down to the seashore. The villagers had woken to a stench that had crept in through their windows; a rotten, sickening stench, the like they'd never smelt before.

"Come on P5. I want you to join hands. This poor fish tried to make it home but got beached in the narrows."

"Is he dead, Miss?"

"Yes, I'm afraid he is, John."

Lucinda felt a ferocious heat grip her plastic sandals, as they danced around the monster whale now rotting in the sun.

Later that day their teacher made them make papier-mache models of it, while Lucinda silently vowed never to go into the sea again – a promise she would keep until some three years later. In the meantime escapism felt safer, closer to home, and so she became a bookworm.

It all began with Enid Blyton's adventure series, the 'Famous Five', but being Lucinda, things quickly took a darker turn. She was attracted to James Herbert's horror book 'The Rats' and, knowing her strictly religious Mother would wholly disapprove, realised she'd have to hide it.

Lucinda hid it in a big old chest in her parent's bedroom, where they kept their woollen jumpers. Now that summer was in full swing, she reckoned it would be a while before they'd go in there again.

One night her parent's decided on an 'early night' and had got there before her. Such was Lucinda's need to devour the next chapter, she decided to sneak in quietly on all fours. Sliding like a snake through the brown shag pile carpet, her eyes slowly adjusted to the dark.

The first thing she noticed above the flickering flames, was the little tub of Vaseline that always sat meltingly warm there. She had often wondered about that little jar, and now to her horror she learned the horrible truth. There they were. Quite the horrible vision. Letting out little groans, little cries for help. What on earth was happening? Were they sharing the same nightmare? Maybe they did everything together? Lucinda's mind was racing. Then she caught sight of her Father on top of her mother. She suddenly couldn't move a muscle and was forced to stay there for quite some time, as they sweated, wrestling amongst the bedding. Finally recovering her senses, she crawled out backwards, grazing both knees with impressive carpet burns. No need for James Herbert that night.

She fought a restless battle with sleep. What else would she discover about them, and the complexities of family life?

A new day dawned, with the walls creaking, and angular flashes of sunlight.

"Are you getting up soon, Lucinda?" Her mother's voice carried shrilly from next door, though that day Lucinda found it hard to meet her mother's gaze or carry on the usual banter with her father. Why did she feel a stranger in her own home? Why did she have an aching urge to run away?

CHAPTER ONE

PART TWO:

NEVER LEAVE HOME
WHEN YOU ARE STILL A CHILD

Lucinda and her best friend Ellery were giggling in class, which to all was nothing unusual, only they seemed to be bubbling with a strange excitement they smugly needed to share. Ellery flicked a rolled-up piece of paper, which bounced off Hazel Manson's head. The girl quickly spun around, her lizard green eyes demanding an explanation. Ellery tilted her chair back and rocked back and forth, teetering on two legs.

"Hey. I just wanted to tell you that this seems like a really good day to die."

You're mad, and you know what? I hope you do, so there."

The school bell sounded, and there was the usual scramble to get out of the door first only this time Lucinda paused to take one final, wistful look back at the place that had been her prison. This would mean goodbye to all of that, to her class and her school lessons, forever.

The rush of freedom propelled the giggling pair out of the school gates and up a steep climb to rolling hills and woodland. Ellery threw her school bag over a high wall first.

"We won't be needing these anymore," she said matter-of-factly, with her trademark low giggle.

"Nope," echoed Lucinda, heaving hers. The contents of their precious school bags took flight like a flock of paper seagulls. That single vision would stay with them both for years to come, as would the empowering sense of freedom.

"What have you brought for eating?"

"I've brought a tin of beans."

"Well I've brought biscuits."

"What, no bread?"

"I suppose it's better than nothing."

They tramped on, bare knees scratched by the hidden thorns amongst the rushes.

"Do you suppose our mothers will be missing us by now?" Lucinda asked quietly, thinking in flashbacks to the horrors she'd witnessed in her parents bedroom just nights before.

"Miss us?. My dad will bloody kill me if I ever see him again."

The wood, which had been tempting and inviting in the sun, now closed darkly around them. There were creaks and cracks in the distance. So many unexplained sounds. Buttery light faded to purple, and without words, the girls joined hands. Lucinda could hear her grandmother's voice, bringing so many threatening images to mind.

"What time is it?"

"Why? Don't tell me you're worried we might meet up with Willie Winkie!"

"Don't be crazy. I'm more worried we might meet up with 'black Danny.' Mum says he's a flasher and an alcoholic."

"What's a flasher?"

"I think it's someone who likes to show off their money."

Suddenly there was a snap behind them, some way off. They locked eyes, and without needing to shout 'Run!' the pair took off at a gallop.

It was quite an exhilarating release from the tension that had been building, and they giggled in sync with their knock-kneed run, school ties whipping their shoulders. On like a couple of gazelles being hunted by lions, jet propelled down the mole infested hill.

"Where to now?" Ellery asked Lucinda, who was bent double, gasping for air.

"I don't know, but I'd feel safer down the shore."

"Good idea, and at least we'll be nearer to catch the ferry in the morning."

It felt colder there. There were clouds of midges, and the washed-up scent of dried seaweed and raw sewage combined.

"Oh no!" Ellery squealed, "There are bats about!"

"Oh, they won't hurt you."

"Wanna bet? I once was riding my bike at speed, and one got tangled in my hair. It was horrible. The stuff of nightmares."

"We could just call it off and walk each other home," Lucinda said quietly. Even in the twilight, she noticed the massive relief, the weight lifting off her friend's shoulders.

Ellery walked Lucinda up to her parent's front door. Lucinda's mind raced as the door inched open and the light blazed out, scattering clouds of directionless insects. She hadn't expected to cry, or run straight into her mother's skirts, burying her head; nor had she expected to see her mother's pained expression, a powerful look she'd never seen before. It was the first time they'd truly bonded, but in seconds her mother pulled away, regaining her stern composure.

"I'll get my coat and walk Ellery home. Lucinda, go straight to bed. We'll talk about this in the morning."

"Bye." Lucinda waved Ellery off, and didn't see her friend for another month. The punishment bit hard over the weeks that followed. No after-school clubs. No tennis or sport. No friends round. Perhaps worst of all, she missed the demolition of an old American air raid shelter that had been standing since the second world war. It was quite the event in the village calendar and would be talked about for years to come. As usual, Lucinda felt the outsider, as the crushing vibrations carried for miles.

CHAPTER TWO

ONLY TAKE PRESCRIPTION MEDICATION

"Lucinda, what are you doing tonight?"

"Practising guitar in my bedroom."

"Why don't you go out with your friends any more? This being locked away night after night just isn't healthy."

"What do you mean? You used to want me to stay in more."

"I know, but now you're fifteen, nearly sixteen, and you should be out enjoying life. You know, meeting girls and boys your own age. Going out dancing, enjoying life," she mouthed angrily, which didn't suit the sentiment at all.

"I am enjoying life," Lucinda snapped, and ran upstairs two at a time.

Her bedroom door slammed, and soon a familiar samba beat began throbbing. The Brazilian music soothed her. She couldn't explain why, but it was her new guilty pleasure, and she'd regularly tune in. It was vaguely sexy, exotic, and about a million miles from the dullness of home. When she did go out, she spitefully hung out with a very different crowd. They tuned into reggae music, had braided long hair, and trailed around looking tired in their Afghan coats.

"Hey, you want to try some magic mushrooms?" asked Joy, the local minister's daughter.

"Why?" Lucinda answered innocently. "I hate the taste of mushrooms. Disgusting!" She pulled a face.

"Oh, we don't eat them. Just watch. We boil them up and make tea."

Lucinda was engrossed in the whole ceremony, from the BobMarley track to the scraping and drying out of the fungi in tinfoil.

"Look," said Joy, "Fiona's got the symbol tattooed on her wrist in henna."

"Latin name: Psilocybe Mexicana."

Lucinda was drawn in hypnotically. Not only by the excitement of dabbling in this seemingly edgy experiment, but feeling truly alive for the second time since discovering music and the hypnotic rhythms from Brazil. She imagined what her mother would think if she could see her now, which made it even more appealing and grown up.

Everything turned hazy. Fiona sipped from her cup first. Lucinda noticed her face turn paler, in startling contrast to her vivid black eyeliner.

"Now your turn."

She swallowed deeply and stared at the lights. They popped and fizzled like fireworks and the patterned carpet was moving. Drawers were popping open of their own accord, and out flew jumpers and socks. Lucinda was reeling, but time was moving on.

"I'd better get home, you guys. Will either of you walk me?"

Joy had passed out and was already snoring. As for Fiona, she gave her a red-eyed "No," pulled her coat around her shoulders and curled up into a ball.

Lucinda began the frightening journey home, afraid to look up at the street lights. Her heart was pounding, but she just had to get through the door.

"You enjoyed yourself, dear?" Her mother asked.

"Yes, it was okay."

She slumped down in her usual chair in front of the television – only that was the only 'norm' in the whole sordid set-up, because her mother was now half human, half pig, with hairy pink pointed ears and an enormous snout. By some miracle she was deftly knitting, furiously peeping over fragile rimmed spectacles, and her red-haired father was luckily asleep, because he was a silky green cockerel.

"Keep a lid on this, Lucinda," she silently preached. "This is all in your fucked up imagination. You're hallucinating on the mushroom brew, but you'll snap out of it soon enough."

Despite appearing a grotesque pig in a floral dress, her mother had truly blossomed, and made happy little grunts and snorts as her favourite Saturday night dancing competition finally got underway.

"Aren't the dresses beautiful Lucinda?"

"Yes. I suppose they are."

"Aren't you going to mention our new colour television? I thought you might have made some comment."

They had been living in a sepia, black and white world for as long as Lucinda had watched television, but of course she had been afraid to comment on anything that night. It took four more hours to come back down off the drug that had stimulated her beyond her wildest imagination but, mind well and truly blown, of course Lucinda had to experience it again, only well away from her parents this time.

She chose a sunny day for a seemingly innocent walk along the shore road, but she felt a bit of a bandito as she hot-footed it to a well-known woody spot where she knew that strain of mushroom had been thriving. Great clumps clung under a rock face, and in no time, Lucinda had ripped off a good couple of bunches. She threw down her jacket, and sat on a warm pebbly ledge, to make her roll-up cigarette filled with the magic mushrooms. Once lit, she inhaled deeply, and she was again transported from one world to another.

She had the privilege of seeing Moses in long beard and biblical dress before her. He raised his staff, and the bush beside him caught fire. It seemed to blaze for hours.

"Wow." Lucinda was coming back down, genuinely believing she had witnessed a miracle, until someone shouting distracted her.

"Look out, dear! The ferry's coming into the pier!" She woke up as water gently splashed her face. She had nearly drowned, but it had been the greatest feeling of peace and contentment she'd ever encountered.

Although Lucinda had once again withdrawn from the colourful crowd she'd been hanging with, her dabbling and lone experimentation nearly ended it all. It typically happened with her parents away from the house one weekend.

"Why don't you come with us?" Her mother had begged.

"I'll be fine, really."

With a list of dos and don'ts ringing in her ears, Lucinda finally had the house all to herself. She put on a dreamy instrumental track and threw more coals on the fire. She idly got up and poured herself a whiskey from her father's cocktail cabinet. a new habit she'd been covering up. She was alone, and could do what she liked.

She made herself comfortable in front of the roaring fire and began meticulously going through her mother's medicine box. There were the usual headache pills and syrupy cough medicines in sickly colours; then there was, expecting miracles to overcome her weak will. She held them up to the light.

"I wonder what will happen if I take some of those?" The whiskey hit hard, and she settled into her experiment.

Lucinda must've swallowed a strip of over thirty before she recovered her senses. By then, things happened fast. She felt ice cold. Her eyes flickered quickly side to side, until she could barely focus. It came with an ominous feeling of dread. Things were going to end badly. With her heart thumping loudly in her chest, and her mouth crying out for water, she staggered up the stairs to bed, but before passing out, she had to leave her mother some sort of explanation, at the very least, a final loving last goodbye. So, it took her all her strength to heave herself up off the pillow, and she began scribbling on her pink bedroom wall. That was it. She lay back down to die. Darkness tightened around her, and a loss of consciousness followed, till she heard the noise of her parent's returning home .

"I'm saved."

Lucinda blacked out again. When she woke next, light was creeping in under her curtains. She could hear her parent's snoring in the room next to hers.

"I've got to stand up." She staggered unsteadily towards her little French windows and peered down to the gravel drive glistening below. Eddie, the local mechanic, was working under the bonnet of her father's car.

She wanted to bang on the windows and shout for help. Instead, she closed the curtains tightly, and stumbled back to bed. She had to wake her parents, like it or not. It was the only way she'd survive this.

"Lucinda, is that you? Why are you knocking?"

"I've taken some pills, I'm not very well."

She heard a disturbance from her parent's bedroom. Her mother appeared in her dressing gown.

"You've just had a bad dream, that's all."

"No, listen. If you don't believe me, look in my jeans pocket. You'll find the empty packet in there."

She could barely see her shocked reaction, but heard her waking her father and running down the stairs. She called the G. P., despite it being the middle of the night.

"Yes, around thirty."

"I see. Make her sick."

In no time her mother had her by the scruff of the neck and was shovelling salt water down her throat. Lucinda retched from the pit of her stomach. Her father appeared in pyjamas and outdoor shoes, a sure sign they were a family in crisis.

"Dad. What's wrong with your car?" she asked between the vile contractions.

"Nothing, Lucinda, why?"

"It's just that Eddie is out there fixing it."

Her mother and father exchanged weary looks that said it all.

"Come on Lucinda. Let's get you back to bed. It's probably best you sleep this off. We'll talk about it in the morning."

Turns out it was far from over, reaching the top of the stairs, reality hit, when she claimed she saw her neighbour's heads popping out of their chimney pots. So, her mother marched her around until the hallucinations calmed, and she slept soundly for another twelve hours.

Of course, she received a lecture from her parents. Worse still, a telling-off by the local doctor. Lucinda overheard him discussing things with her mother as he marched out carrying his leather case.

"I recommend she see a psychologist. Carry on like this and she'll not reach twenty-one." It was just another rule she had to follow and, cruelly, a journey she was forced to make alone.

It was on that lonely bus and train ride to meet with her psychologist, some forty miles, that Lucinda puzzled over why her mother hadn't come with her. There was a coldness, a strange disconnect that Lucinda had recognised from a young age. There were few motherly hugs to be had, and if she held her hand, it was only 'til they had crossed a busy road. As soon as they reached the other side, her hand would immediately drop like a stone.

Those reflections carried with her into the health centre's waiting room, where a large crowd had gathered. Some children were waiting on their dental appointments, and a gang of teenage boys were nervously awaiting sexual health results. Lucinda sat beside the dental crowd, too ashamed to approach the receptionist's desk. Gradually the waiting room emptied, and Lucinda was left sitting alone.

"Are you waiting to see Doctor Baird?" the receptionist asked, craning her neck.

"Yes," she answered quietly

Lucinda visited four rooms during her examination. First, a woman showed her a pack of cards, all with different images, and she had to answer what was first to come into her mind. She then had to copy pages of symbols. It was all very clinical and strange by the time she got to meet Doctor Baird, a fat, wrinkly man who reminded her of a toad.

She sat down and burst into tears. He offered her a tissue. All he had asked was, "Why are you here?" It was a conundrum within a conundrum, and as unfathomable as life itself. He might as well have asked, "Why were you born?"

Where could she go from here? She faced a bleak future. She had been crying out for help, but no one was listening.

Lucinda felt empty on the rattling ride home, with commuters returning from their offices. In the weeks and months that followed, a social worker called. It was summer, and her mother would get out her best China to entertain her on the lawn. Lucinda seemed to be superfluous to the whole occasion, and would throw a ball back and forth for their neighbour's dog while listening into snippets of their conversation.

"It's nice to see a success story at last. She seems to have settled down, thanks to you and your husband."

Her mother ran with the plaudits whilst Lucinda carried on the self-harm.

There were other changes to her body, apart from those vicious looking scars. Her hormones were suddenly in overdrive, and she began taking an interest in good looking boys. Ellery's brother John came into her sights. He was tall, a couple of years older, with piercing blue eyes, a flashing white smile, and a penchant for rolling perfectly thin cigarettes. He taught her all she needed to know about the mechanics of owning a moped, and generally love making happened in the great outdoors; at one with nature.

Nettles and wasp stings, and a raft of magic mushrooms, perhaps carried Lucinda on her greatest journey of all, when she travelled all the way inside a tall chestnut tree, visiting on a flowing river of sap all the way from root to branches. She popped back out into glorious sunshine, feeling a sense of true contentment and spirituality, beautifully calm.

So, she continued to dodge death, despite her best efforts, and finally she connected with music again. Through a friend of a friend, she was introduced to a fellow musician. He'd described him as "a good guy from the big smoke."

"He's just moved into the village and is looking for others to jam with. Would you be interested, Lucinda?"

"Sure. Why not?"

She didn't think much more about it, until one night he appeared on their doorstep. Her father played in a little band, had heard about him and invited him along.

"Lucinda, meet Mike. He's a bass player and has come to join us this session."

CHAPTER THREE

PART ONE:

ONLY EVER MARRY FOR LOVE

Lucinda watched Mike unzip the cover of his bass guitar. It was a statement, full-bellied, shiny and black. He wasn't classically handsome, but nonetheless he had piercing blue eyes, and a smile a mile wide.

They began their session effortlessly, and Mike's professional bassline transformed the band's music. Over the weeks that followed, Lucinda and Mike became firm friends with so much in common.

"Hey, Lucinda. I'm going to see a big band perform in the city at the Ironhorse bar. Care to join me?"

"Sure. Why not?" she answered casually, shrugging her shoulders, despite her heart nearly thumping out of her chest.

The city cast a spell on Lucinda from the minute she stepped into that zipped-up, glazed, chaotic world. She was mesmerised by the snail trail of traffic, from black taxis to red double-decker buses, the crowds all tearing in different directions, and pigeons swarming in clouds.

The Ironhorse bar was very atmospheric. The stench of alcohol hit you at the door. The band was tuning up their instruments. Trumpets let out elephant roars, and the drummer stood up to crack every cymbal. He had a towel around his neck and meant business.

They sank into a corner table and Mike ordered drinks. Lucinda chose vodka and lime on ice. With the big band swinging away in the corner, it was all very grown up, and very far from the village she'd grown up in. It soon became a regular thing, only their feelings quickly deepened. Making eye contact caused sparks to fly. It was a magical moment, because Lucinda knew they were destined to be together.

"Move in with me," Mike begged over the weeks and months that followed.

"I can't. What about my mother?"

"What about her?" Mike giggled sexily. "I'd rather make room in my life for you."

"You know how religious she is. She would never agree to it. She calls it 'living in sin.'"

"What's so sinful about being in love?"

They made temporary measures of meeting her half-way. Lucinda and Mike would spend every evening together. They'd climb into bed like a regular married couple, then would wake to a shrill alarm clock that woke them at three a.m. Lucinda would bid the milkman good morning, as she snuck in through the front door and ran silently to bed. Occasionally her mother would give a quiet cough, just to let her know she was still awake and was logging her arrival on her bedside digital clock.

Overtime, it took its toll on them both. Mike's complexion faded from rosy to white. Lucinda was pale grey and took to her bed to have regular 'top-up' afternoon naps.

"Why don't we get married?" Mike asked one day, out of the blue.

"Yes, but you'll have to come and ask my father's permission. Hang up and come over and ask him now."

Lucinda paced, sensing a storm brewing. Indoors, life ticked on as normal. Her mother was in her favourite armchair, happily knitting, and her father was carefully placing more logs on the fire like any good boy scout. Lucinda waited to see Mike's car arriving, but her nervous breath quickly steamed up the glass door. Finally, she heard his car door slam. The doorbell, normally so welcoming and demure, sounded like a car alarm, real glass-shattering. The next few moments happened like a strange, shared out of body experience. Beads of sweat popped up on Mike's forehead.

"Hey, Mike. Come on in and have a seat."

Lucinda knew her father was fond of him. But nothing could have prepared them for his reaction when the bombshell spilled out of Mike's mouth. "I have fallen in love with Lucinda, and would like us to get married. Do I have your blessing?"

Lucinda's father dragged himself forward to the very edge of his chair. He reached angrily for a pack of cigarettes, despite having recently given up smoking.

"Richard!" Her mother's knitting pins fell at her side. "Aren't you at least going to offer your congratulations?"

"Ah well, I don't know about that. I mean, I knew you were getting along well, but you hardly know each other."

"You proposed to mum within months!"

"Well, yes, that's right, but this is different."

Lucinda felt drained, to the point she felt like some useless commodity that they were fighting over.

The fire roared like never before, because her father had a need to stoke it that night, despite being drenched in sweat. There was a wailing and gnashing of teeth, but happily, thanks to lengthy discussions, Lucinda's parents slowly came around to the whole idea of a family wedding taking place around the middle of May. Her mother even went along with the idea of a registry office ceremony, with only twelve others present.

From that day on, Lucinda felt freer than she'd ever been before. Her home was her own. There were no more outdated rules to follow, from her teachers, her parents, or even the shackles of God.

CHAPTER THREE

PART TWO:

NEVER LEAVE YOUR HUSBAND IN
THE MIDDLE OF THE NIGHT

Ten years of marriage flew past in the happy blink of an eye. Lucinda and Mike were a textbook couple, who shared the exact same passions in life.

One day, however, things took a different turn. Lucinda had been tidying the house, and was finishing straightening her curtains, when a pirate-black cloud appeared to split the sky. There was a rumble in the distance and thunder rolled in. Her elderly neighbour was struggling to push a lawn mower up and down a tiny rectangle of grass. Her husband had recently died, and so it was yet another task she had to manage now she was on her own. The striking image suddenly brought Lucinda's own life sharply into focus.

"What if Mike were to die?" she mused. That could happen anytime. It struck her then, that she hated where they had been living. It was far too suburban. No privacy at all. Worse still, she hated the village. It was a soulless, dead, one-horse town. Then, to her horror, in that light-bulb moment, she announced to her own private audience that she no longer loved Mike. In pleasing everyone, she had slowly lost herself again, and was trapped in a loveless marriage. Mike had represented freedom, back then; a whole new exciting world lay before her. They had lived and breathed that life for so long, but without music, they had very little in common. Lucinda wanted to be free, to explore the world, whilst Mike was hankering after early retirement, to play summer seasons in the Spanish Costa clubs. She had steadfastly decided that they should talk things over, but knew in her heart of hearts they had been going through the motions for a very long time.

They immediately decided to take a holiday. Not a working one, or to anywhere they'd been before. Just something different, to see if they could get back on track.

Weeks later they were packing for Portugal, and the rocky, azure coastline of the spectacular Algarve. What they didn't know, as their plane touched down at Faro International Airport, was that they were landing at an important time in the Portuguese calendar: New Year's Eve. A time of magical tradition, fizzling fireworks, and pomp and circumstance.

Just having bounced their suitcases up the stairs of their whitewashed hotel, with its balconies laden with colourful bougainvillea, they learned that on the 1st of January they should: dive into the ocean; dance around a tree to attract prosperity; and jump three times on one leg, whilst holding a glass of champagne, at the stroke of midnight – not forgetting to eat raisins to have wishes granted.

It was a breathless introduction and felt magical from the start, like all your birthdays and Christmases rolled into one. Mike pulled Lucinda onto their unmade mattress, and they rolled around laughing. Seconds later someone was slipping a note under their door.

"Management invite you to join us in the ballroom tonight at eleven o'clock, whereupon you will have a green cabbage soup, a tradition in Portugal at New Year. You will also drink 'diesel', a very special cocktail."

Lucinda pulled a face as Mike read on. It was strange, but clearly they were going to have fun there. Fireworks fizzled over the roof tiles as they began getting dressed. Arriving in the packed hotel's foyer earlier that day, they had got on nodding terms with another couple from Nottingham.

"They look like an interesting pair," Mike had commented under his breath. "They both look very **arty**."

Right on cue, they banged into them again, as music came pumping from the ballroom.

"Are you going in?" Mike asked, flicking his head in the general direction of the ballroom. "Oh, and pleased to meet you. We're Mike and Lucinda."

"We're going to check the band out."

"We're actually musicians ourselves." Lucinda took a step back into the shadows, cringing ever so slightly at the regular boast.

"I'm Gregg, and this is Pauline. We're good mates. We're in the same year at art college. It's holiday time, and we were both at a loose end. So that's about it in a nutshell. Here we are!" The four of them headed towards the ballroom. "You'll probably not enjoy the music, then," Gregg added, ducking his head to get through the door. "I've heard they're a couple of alcoholics."

"Then they'll be good," Mike stated simply, causing a couple of raised eyebrows. They soon got separated, busting strange shapes on the dance floor. For some reason, it seemed the management also deemed it compulsory for every reveller to be adorned with Hawaiian garlands around their necks upon arrival.

There was a giant clock counting down the time in one corner, beside a long table where the green cabbage soup was being hurriedly served into ceramic bowls.

"Hey, Mike," Gregg yelled from the opposite end of their bench. "Take it easy when trying the diesel. Just be careful, remember, small sips. It's been known to knock men flat on their backs."

"Then line them up. Lucinda's Scottish!"

As the magical hour approached, Lucinda knocked back the potent diesel, washed it down with the rustic cabbage broth, and the table widened considerably.

"Let's dance." She pulled Mike up by his tie, but before long he had joined another table, and was soon playing darts with a stranger. Gregg slipped out of his seat, and they were suddenly rubbing shoulders. "Where's Pauline?"

"She's got a migraine, so she's gone for an early night to sleep it off."

"That's too bad."

"I know, but there's always tomorrow. I've been watching you two."

"Mm. What do you mean, exactly?"

"Well, when you're out walking, like when we passed you on those hired bikes this afternoon, just as you were arriving," Lucinda had been nervously rubbing the rim of her empty glass, so vigorously that it suddenly squealed above the music, "your husband walks way in front of you, and tonight, he's paying more attention to that woman than he is to you. How does that make you feel?"

Lucinda's cheeks burned furiously under the white laser strobe. She shrugged her shoulders and tried to laugh it off. "Mike's a party animal. He just loves other people's company, that's all. I guess I'm more of a shrinking violet."

"Don't put yourself down, Lucinda. You're a very beautiful and talented young woman Mike's told me all about how gifted you are."

Midnight shattered their quiet moment alone and gold glitter rained from the ceiling. Lucinda was high on diesel fumes and didn't care who knew it. An hour passed. Then Mike came over to announce he was ready to leave early.

"Well, I'm not," she answered defiantly.

"Okay then. You do what you want." He made an angry exit through the saloon style wooden doors, but Lucinda didn't care, she was flying.

Gregg grabbed her onto the dance floor, and they seemed to be spinning right through one another's bodies. She could see him with her eyes closed, almost as if he'd snatched her very soul. He suddenly bent and kissed her.

"Happy New Year, Lucinda."

'It was electric. Sparks flew, and from that moment she knew she was in love. Despite them only being there for a day there were accusing fingers pointing at the pair, disapproving gestures, and whispers especially from the group Mike had spent the evening with.

"Come on, Lucinda. I'll walk you to your apartment."

"Mike will be waiting up. He might be worried."

They began to whisper as they neared her door. "Thanks for your company tonight. You've been a breath of fresh air. A true free spirit. I should know, because it takes one to know one. Hey look, your number is Pauline's and mine backwards. You're two three zero, and we're zero three two. I knew this place was magical. It must be a sign." He bent and boldly kissed her, and it turned her inside out and flipped her against the wall. Pauline's door clicked gently closed on the floor below. She had been listening all along.

Lucinda fell into bed fully clothed, and was unconscious until someone knocking wakened her.

"I'll go," said Mike.

She heard voices echoing from out in the hall, then in stepped Gregg. Things were suddenly frighteningly real. Why had he come? What was about to happen? Snippets of the night before crashed in around her, though there wasn't time to work her story out. She had to try and behave has if nothing had happened. Her reputation depended upon it. With her heart visibly beating out of her chest, she boldly made her entrance in her towelling robe.

"Hi, how are you feeling this morning?"

"Not bad, I suppose, considering the weird concoction of a witches brew we swallowed."

It was all so very civilised, and yet at the same time so incredibly wrong. They chatted, made plans for the following days, and then he left like some higher force with an invisible shield around him and, with a satisfied smile a mile wide, secretly winked in her direction.

"Nice bloke."

"Yes, very. Pauline seems very nice too."

"Oh, I've invited them both to come for a holiday. They said they'd love to take me up on the offer."

CHAPTER THREE

PART THREE:

NEVER LEAVE YOUR HUSBAND IN THE MIDDLE OF THE NIGHT

It was Saturday morning, and Lucinda found herself home alone, with Mike out golfing. She had decided to have a lazy morning, and was still in her towelling bathrobe with comic strip sheep pyjamas come ten o'clock.

The phone sounded shrilly in the downstairs hallway. It'll be for Mike, about some gig or another, she thought, and decided to ignore it, biting loudly into an apple and sliding into their silky bedsheets. It rang again, and then at regular intervals, like some desperate code that simply wasn't about to let go. Suddenly, the penny dropped.

"Oh my God, it's Gregg." She threw her apple onto the floor and ran down the stairs at a gallop.

"Hi Lucinda. How are you? I knew you were home. What about Mike?"

"Out golfing."

"I'm coming to visit you, Lucinda, in two weeks. Pauline can't come, she's working. Look, I can't wait to see you. I've missed you like crazy."

"Me too, but won't Mike be suspicious?"

"Suspicious of what? A New Year's kiss at midnight? Come on, it's important you stay strong. You must trust me."

Two weeks later and the stage was set. Mike and Lucinda were waiting on the bustling platform for Gregg's train to arrive. Mike was wearing his best suit and tie and was holding a camera belt wrapped tightly around his wrist.

"Here he comes, Lucinda. Can't wait to show him around. You can make him one of your famous slap-up meals, and we'll take him to the Ironhorse tomorrow."

Lucinda spotted Gregg through steam and smoke as the guardsman blew his whistle. The men exchanged hearty bear hugs, but Lucinda smiled and stepped back shyly.

The next morning the mood cranked up a notch. They were back in the city, feeling about to burst.

"This is some city. You guys must be super proud." Gregg was acting like a cross between an American tourist and an over-excited schoolboy. His camera seemed to ricochet off every street and angular building, and he was constantly asking them to strike an embarrassing pose that got them noticed for all the wrong reasons.

Lucinda felt a wave of relief wash over her when they entered the Ironhorse hallway and the familiar stench of liquor and smoke hit her like a friendly slap on the back. In fact, Lucinda's popularity was now slightly higher than Mike's, since he'd introduced her. There were few other women who frequented the pub, or took any part in the hard-nosed jazz scene, so she'd become something of a local legend.

As they were a little late in arriving, the band struck up immediately, the power nearly knocking Gregg back in his chair. The orchestra buried a few well-known classics before the extraordinarily rowdy Saturday crowd were on their feet, clapping along.

It was only on the second verse of the well-known standard, a tune entitled 'Luck be a Lady', that Lucinda realised Gregg was squeezing one of her buttocks by way of keeping time. She wasn't the only one to have noticed. The twenty-one-piece orchestra's band leader was also plainly frowning at the shocking sight. He shook his head, deliberately laid down his baton, and retreated to the gent's toilets. The sexual chemistry between Lucinda and Gregg could have powered the band and the musicians into the wee hours, if their nerves had been able to stand it. Instead, the three left on a high to catch their train shortly before the set ended.

The next day Mike was back to work, leaving Lucinda and Gregg alone. They hugged and kissed, taking care to always hide from prying eyes behind the curtains, but as the day went on Lucinda dropped her guard and, when out on a well-known walking trail, had dragged an unsuspecting Gregg into a pile of bushes, where it all got hot and steamy. They emerged, looking every inch a pair who'd been dragged through a hedge backwards and up to no good, and banged right into Lucinda's mother's best friend, who was out walking her dog.

"Hello," Lucinda said briskly as they passed her by. The poor woman tried to answer, but simply side-stepped them and smiled awkwardly.

"I think we got away with that." They hugged tightly and giggled.

So, the day rolled into night, and Mike returned home. He was tired and went off to bed early, urging Gregg to trawl through their holiday photos, of which he was rightly proud. Gregg had brought a couple of photo albums of his own, though, and his looked fresh and exciting: scenes from Istanbul's old quarter, and snapshots of real life from all around the world.

Lucinda was captivated. This was the life she'd been craving all along. On went her favourite Brazilian music, and they rubbed hips and danced passionately with Mike snoring loudly upstairs.

Around two o'clock in the morning, as the volume had inched up a notch, Mike came running downstairs in his checked jockey y-fronts, much to Lucinda's horror and Gregg's amazement.

"What's going on, you two?" His words echoed. He looked a comical, yet tragic fool.

"Shall I tell him?" Lucinda asked in a shocking instant. Gregg reeled back, knowing what was about to come. It was two-thirty in the morning, pitch black outside, and big fluffy snowflakes were beginning to stick and slide in pretty patterns down their windows.

"Tell me what? Come on Lucinda, you'd better spit it out."

She glanced across at Gregg, who'd turned pale and ghostly. The shocking moment had sobered him up. "I don't love you any more. I love Gregg, and we're leaving."

"Is that it, then? Is that all you've got to say for yourself?" Gregg was obviously waiting for the sucker punch, but instead Mike announced they'd better get pissed together.

"You go on up and grab a couple of hours sleep," Gregg quietly urged her. "I'll stay here with Mike. See you in the morning."

When morning finally came, it was Gregg staring down at her. "Come on, Lucinda. We'd better get going."

The snow had worked its magic overnight, leaving the village sparkling and glistening like a jewellery box. It had eerily dampened all sounds, except for the strains of Mike snoring ahead of a crushing hangover.

Oddly, as they waited in the biting cold, Lucinda was feeling nostalgic about her one-time prison of a village. She also knew, as they waited for their bus to arrive, that it would never belong to her again.

Several months later, she and Gregg were making plans to return and collect her belongings. Mike had been phoning Lucinda on a regular basis, asking what he should tell the neighbours. Typical suburban drama that had to be played out and not buried. She felt she had to return, not only to collect some of her possessions, but to put a line under their marriage, so they could both move on.

An old college friend had kindly offered to put her and Gregg up for a night in her flat. It was half-way between the city and home, and they could be in either in under an hour.

"Stop fretting Lucinda. Let's not make it all bad. We'll go to the Ironhorse in the afternoon, if the big band are playing. Then you can go see Mike and do what you need to. I'll stay with Kate till you're ready to leave. Just ring me when you're ready."

She felt nervous approaching her own home a stranger, and an even bigger fool nervously tapping at her own front door. Mike opened it up straight away. He'd obviously been pacing. He was wearing her favourite aftershave and had dressed to impress. The smell of their favourite meal was wafting from the slow cooker, and it was painfully obvious this was a carefully planned scene of seduction that clearly wasn't going to end well.

"Come in. You look great, Lucinda. Sit down. Take your coat off, and tell me what you've been up to."

He'd obviously practised the opening chat-up lines. He was smiling, and yet his brow was creased and anxious. He could have stretched the small talk further, but just had to spit it out.

"Lucinda, are you coming back to me? I've been going crazy here alone, rattling around the house. I've never been so lonely. I haven't spoken to any of our crowd in ages."

"No, Mike. I'm only here to collect my things. If you don't mind, I'd like to go get them from our bedroom."

The mood turned shades darker. She was worried for her safety and began grabbing a random pile of clothes. Mike was suddenly in the room beside her, leaning over her menacingly, shouting and lecturing her about what a good life she was leaving, and how if she left, she was never to darken his door again. She began dialling Gregg's number.

"That's right. Go ahead and tell lover boy."

Mike had lost it completely. He frightened her, and there was no telling what he was about to do next. Lucinda ducked under his muscly arm, ran out of the bedroom, and down the stairs as fast as she could. He was right behind her when she picked up her guitar.

"You're not taking that, lady. I gave you that as a present."

"Okay. Then I'll take your bass guitar instead."

"Oh no you won't, you selfish bitch." There was an ugly tussle in the hallway, just as Kate's little metro pulled up outside. Lucinda summoned all her strength in anger and tore the bass guitar out of Mike's hand. Mike ran out behind her into the street and the curtains twitched. He finally had his performance. Lucinda threw her belongings into the backseat of her friend's car, with Mike's flailing body making strides to catch up. Only then did Lucinda notice the green 'L' plate in the rear window, as his angry red face loomed large.

"Please tell me you've passed your driving test?"

"Oh yes, don't worry. Now let me see. Jiggle the gear stick," she muttered, "in with the clutch."

"Dear God, please hurry, Kate." Just as his fat hand touched the back of the car, they exploded off in a cloud of black diesel like Batman and Robin. What a memory. What a sad ending, yet so fittingly funny, as they bunny-hopped up to the only junction in town.

CHAPTER FOUR

NEVER TRUST A STRANGER
WHEN YOU'RE FAR FROM HOME

For a few weeks Lucinda felt in limbo, still reeling with guilt over leaving Mike and her father, so fragile and soon after the sudden death of her mother. Gregg intuitively sensed her mood, and out of the blue suggested they should travel.

"Hey Lucinda. Come with me to the library. A woman with your talent should be able to make money anywhere in the world."

"What exactly do you mean?"

"Well, I've been in Paris, and happen to know the government pays buskers to play music in the streets. They encourage the arts. It's not frowned upon. You could make a small fortune in Eastern Europe. They go one better, and provide accommodation for writers, and musicians. What have you got to lose, kid? It's a no-brainer for me. See the world and get paid for it."

As the words sank in, she realised this had been her dream all along. The stars had aligned in Portugal, and now she was about to fulfil her destiny. With plans in place, they hurried off to the local library, and that night returned home with a collection of maps. After pouring over them, they booked flights to Budapest and were soon on a bumpy ride with a plane-full of Swiss school children, who cheered every time they hit turbulence.

It felt magical touching down amid the twinkling lights of Budapest, which was draped in mist and fizzed purple, thanks to the dim glow of yellow street lights. Clearly Gregg wasn't such a romantic, as he was flicking through directions to the nearest youth hostel, a stone's throw from the river Danube. He'd raved about the place before they left home, but Lucinda was more fearful now they were part of the action, and alone in the edgy city after dark.

The streets were remarkably empty. Over time they discovered there was a nine o'clock curfew in place and they were facing a hefty fine if discovered. They quickly scuttled indoors. The place felt hostile from the get-go, with a load of unwelcoming signs at reception. It was thirty dollars a night if you shared a room. Without much of a choice they grudgingly accepted and were handed two thin towels before the hatch shut down for the night.

Closing the door behind them, they were finally safe, and could see the funny side. Gregg, the eternal optimist, was busily making plans for the following morning.

"We'll go to the citizens bureau and get all this sorted out," he announced, and the most wonderful thing was that Lucinda believed him.

The sun streamed in early the next morning, and echoing voices joyously filled the corridors, as the guests showered and headed to find breakfast. In their case, it was a couple of warm croissants they bought from a street seller, then it was off to munch them, with their sandals dangling over the slick River Danube.

Joggers passed, and a procession of old men out walking their dogs, before it hit them then that it was Sunday, and nothing much ever happens on a Sunday, no matter where you are in the world.

"We can't afford another night here, babe. What do you want to do? This city is expensive. I mean, once you start earning thing's will be different. I'm just scared if we hang around here too long, this place will swallow us whole."

"You're right as always. What do you suggest?"

"Well, I was talking to a guy in the shower room, and according to him there is one bus out of here today, it takes you to the border crossing and into Romania. I believe it's incredibly cheap there. We'll be able to live like kings!"

Without the pot of gold at the end of the rainbow, they travelled further east, along with a weary, snaking queue of tired traders returning home.

Eventually they found themselves in Istanbul, a cultural clash of east meets west, ancient meets modern.

"Let's find a hotel. Our bodies need to rest. We'll settle in and order breakfast. Apple cay! Oh man, I love that stuff. It's the perfect accompaniment to people watching, and the Bosporus is the perfect place for that."

"You mean you've been here before?"

"Oh yeah, years ago. You know, a family holiday that just happened to drag." Gregg looked a little uncomfortable, but Lucinda let it pass, for good things were about to happen: a sit-down meal, a stand-up wash, and a couple of comfy beds. It seemed they had no sooner tucked into their omelettes, washed down with that tangy apple cay, than Lucinda woke with a jump to probably the most startling sound she'd ever heard. It was early morning prayers being offered to Allah out of a set of speakers attached to the Blue Mosque, and seemingly inches behind her headboard. The wailing sounded all around the city, issuing such a powerful statement of where they were, and how life had altered.

Gregg, oddly, slept through it all, and feeling refreshed they strolled down early evening to sit by the Bosporus Strait, where all manner of boats and barges jockeyed for position. Groups of soldiers and sailors in uniform came and went, leaving loved ones crying and others embracing, a tide of emotions playing out as if part of a film.

The fading sun melted into the shadows, and it became obvious on their stroll through the backstreets to their hotel, sipping a couple of cold beers, that they were being followed. It didn't take long for them to become a target for pickpockets, and all manner of shady individuals who'd invited themselves along. Gregg got out of it calmly, giving a couple the slip by taking a detour through the Red Mosque's lush gardens.

"This place has always had a dangerous edge. I suppose we really should push east again, babe."

"OK, whatever you think's best."

It was a confusing time for Lucinda Grey. In a way, she had all she'd ever wanted, time and the means to explore the world, and it opening before her, but every mile that slipped behind her left her feeling more vulnerable and further from home, and the family she had left behind now only popped out from pages in her diary. The security of being married to Mike had left her feeling chained at times; however, Gregg was the complete opposite, a true free spirit whose mind knew no boundaries.

In a few short dusty hours, they found themselves in Trabzon, a bustling seaport in Eastern Turkey. By then, one hotel looked pretty much like another, so they settled in the Imperial Hotel, on the second floor. It had rickety wooden floors, beautiful rusty ironwork framing the French windows and, best of all, a sea view – if the fog should ever lift.

"Let's rest, then take a walk down to the harbour." Gregg was fast asleep in minutes. Lucinda studied him intently whenever she could.

Later, after he'd slept, they walked the length of the harbour, waving and happily chatting to whoever would listen, from sea Captains to deckhands expertly winding rope. They scattered gulls, and filled their lungs full of salt air, until Gregg stopped abruptly.

"Hey, look, Lucinda. Look at that boat. The flag I mean, at the stern, it's flying the hammer and sickle."

"Yep," she nodded dumbly. "It's Russian. Imagine that. I bet it's a fascinating place, and dirt cheap I bet you. We could live like kings there," she echoed, laughing.

Gregg began planning their next trip, as soon as they returned to their hotel room. He was like an eager puppy on the loose, with boundless energy. The next morning, they woke to unbroken sunshine. The mist had lifted and the sky was piercingly blue. After drinking several cups of tangy apple cay, they were refreshed enough to stroll through Attaturk Park, with its high, leafy cathedral like pathways, and couples strolling arm in arm. It struck Lucinda then that she was the only woman out walking. The couples were all smartly dressed men.

After a bit of smart talking, Gregg managed to persuade the powers that be at the Russian consulate to issue them with three months Georgian business visas, on the strength that Lucinda was a well-known British journalist, with a professional interest in that part of the world.

"What do you want to go there for?" Another asked after the main suit stepped out. "They have civil war there. People are starving. Many have been shot and killed."

"Don't listen to him Lucinda. He's just scare-mongering, that's all. Did you see the size of some of these women in our queue? They certainly didn't look starving to me, or in any way nervous to be returning home."

As usual, Gregg seemed right, and he had this reassuring look that always spun her around to his way of thinking. It had become a powerful weapon since embarking on their trip, and if used she'd gladly have followed him to hell and back.

They spent days 'on hold', waiting on the captain to fill their boat. Nights at the Imperial were vaguely exotic, and Lucinda soon learned their hotel was full of Russian prostitutes, who were making appointments to have sex as often as possible, before returning home with enough money to see them through the next Georgian winter. At eight o'clock precisely, hair dryers droned, the water-pipes thumped, and the smell of cheap perfume hung on the stairs. The women then left the corridors and hallways in a moody grey smokescreen, in leather, lace and lacquered hair. It was the ultimate 'Rocky Horror'!

Night three, and the night before they were due to sail, Gregg perched on the end of Lucinda's bed, with the dreaded look of "there's something I need to tell you."

"What's wrong, Gregg? You can tell me anything."

"I know that, babe, but this is a big one, and I want you to hear me out, you understand?"

"Of course." He looked pale, yet sweaty. She'd never seen him looking this unhinged before.

"Lucinda, I married a Georgian woman a few years back."

"You married. You mean you still are?"

"Hush. Stay calm. Wait till I explain things. I married her to get a Russian passport, that's all, I promise. The marriage was never consummated. It was the same for her. She's a teacher and wanted to move to England."

"So is that why you're so desperate to get back to her?"

"No, not at all. Far from it!" He gripped her shoulders, staring powerfully into her eyes. "I love you completely. You're the love of my life. That meant nothing. Just a shared contract, that's all."

A single tear rolled down Lucinda's cheek. What else hadn't he told her? It had taken this long, and they had travelled so far together. What else must he be hiding?

"I just can't understand why you'd want to go back and see her after all this time. Why, Gregg, why?"

The big man's face crumpled. He looked close to tears. "I thought we'd have to stay together for a matter of weeks. Turns out I had to stay married and share the same residence for three years to get a passport. Not easy, when there was zero attraction, and she didn't speak a word of English."

"You fool. You bloody idiot." She punched his muscly arm, then pulled her fingers painfully back into her cardigan sleeve. Lucinda sobbed uncontrollably but was soon giggling at the absurdity of his story. "So how did you explain you were leaving? I suppose you needed an interpreter?"

"That's the shameful thing. I signalled I was going out to buy a loaf of bread, and legged it. A bit like you leaving Mike."

"It's nothing like the situation between me and Mike," she flared up angrily. "Our marriage had been a sham for years. You spotted it when we met in Portugal."

"Okay, Lucinda, I'm sorry. I was scared to return to explain things, because she has six burly brothers who would have hunted me down. Irakley, the eldest, was never cut out to be a soldier, but he is handy with his Kalashnikov rifle, and wouldn't have thought twice about wiping me out. Look, it's a fantastic country, and a big one too. I've no intentions of going anywhere near that family. I made a load of other connections, and I'll be proud to show you off. Don't laugh, but we'll also be rich there.

We'll live like kings – oh, and just one other thing. You know how we exchanged our money in Istanbul?"

"Yes." He already had her attention. "I couldn't understand why we had to exchange it for the American dollar over our own money, and all in single dollar bills."

"The American dollar is more sought after. You wouldn't want to pull out, say, a ten dollar bill in a crowd. They'd murder you for that at the market. It wouldn't be wise." Gregg swallowed hard for the second time that evening. There was more, and the mood was electric. "In the seventies the Americans withdrew their currency as it was practically worthless on the world's stage."

"Yes, but what has that to do with us?" Lucinda blinked back innocently. She felt safer acting the dizzy blonde, with another bombshell about to drop.

"Well, you know how we've been walking around like a couple of padded scarecrows with all our single dollars tucked into our clothes and down our socks?"

"Yes," Lucinda's voice faltered.

"Well, that exchange office clearly saw us coming, and off-loaded a shed-full of outdated dollars on us."

"You mean we're broke?"

"I'm afraid so. We have no choice but to try and pass it off, and hope no one will notice."

"Well that's just great. We're heading to a dangerous place without money and where credit cards don't work to launder money, and you're likely on a mafia hit-list! You're not selling this Gregg. Believe me. Yet there's something magical between us. Always has been. It's crazy, I know, but I trust you, and would follow you to the ends of the earth."

CHAPTER FIVE

NEVER STICK YOUR NOSE IN
SOMEONE ELSE'S WAR

They sped through much of Georgia, travelling mostly at night, completely skipping through the town of Poti, where Gregg's wife and vengeful brothers were still waiting for an explanation. Things felt very tense when they arrived at the border town of Batumi, right on the Georgian-Abkhazian border. Gregg had persuaded an old friend to drive them up to the well-armed crossing, where a handful of civilians had been wiped out by snipers trying to cross the River Inguri the night before. To make matters worse, the sky suddenly looked like an over-ripe watermelon. Pink and black and fit to burst, and as the tension mounted, their driver Butu refused to take them any further.

Thundery rain battered the dusty ground beneath them as his car spun in an angry circle. They were left right there on the empty dirt road, their rucksacks and clothes sodden and hanging off them. Suddenly, out of nowhere a caped Georgian officer stepped forward. He was a giant of a man, with broad shoulders. Lucinda let Gregg do most of the talking. She knew the drill by now. He could charm the birds from the trees when he got going and this was no exception.

"Hey, Lucinda," he yelled loudly, to her horror. "Doesn't this guy remind you of Arnold Schwarzenegger?"

"Yes, he does," she answered shyly.

"A handsome man like you should have your photo taken with the girl. Come on Lucinda, don't be shy, step right up."

Lucinda shot Gregg an alarmed look, but he didn't take any notice. His behaviour was farcical given the seriousness of their situation. Soon other camouflaged soldiers stepped out from the bushes laughing. They were draped in netting and ivy, their powerful rifles casually off shoulder like lady's leather handbags. Clearly, this was no ordinary war.

"Roll up. Roll up. What a bunch of handsome lads! Let's get you all in shot." Gregg dug deep into his rucksack and pulled out packs of Turkish cigarettes he'd brought with them from Trabzon. At least he had the sense not to produce their dodgy dollars!

Many of the soldiers thanked him and lit up, as he charged around, arranging the perfect shot. Lucinda was clearly worried that all this noise and distraction would attract the enemy's attention, and she feared for her life and for Gregg's at the same time, but bravely soldiered on.

As usual Gregg's powerful persuasive aura rubbed off on the captain and he promised them a safe crossing amid their armed guard. Gregg winked at her once they'd reached the other side. The man was on a mission and an unstoppable force.

The captain bent and shared quiet but forceful words in the Abkhazian officer's ear, and miraculously the road barricade lifted. The warring officers stepped back and respectfully saluted.

Gregg and Lucinda were bundled into the head of security's car. A rather flustered looking pale and skinny officer simply introduced himself as Alexander. They bounced around in his backseat for a while, with his Kalashnikov sitting proudly in front. It was a crazy ride, which made it nearly impossible to talk, as they traversed around deadly potholes and bulbous pigs idly lying flat in the road. The news he passed on clearly wasn't good.

"Local fishermen pulled out 27 unexploded mines from the river here last night, and many civilians, including children, have been killed." He'd punctuate the horror at times by locking eyes with Lucinda in his rear-view mirror. A steely blue, determinedly designed to shock her.

Gregg nudged Lucinda's bare legs once they screeched up outside his own head of security building merely a brick hut surrounded by barbed wire.

He barked, "Wait here," and pulled out his walkie-talkie.

"Da, eto Alexander. Hurry up for Christ's sake and open this bloody door."

"He looks scared to death to be out there," quipped Gregg who seemed to be lapping the whole thing up. "Hardly what you'd expect of a British army officer."

The door inched open, and the pair were hurried inside to safety and the rare feeling they had entered another world. As instructed, they sat on a wooden bench in a cool corridor under a white metal fan, which soothed with the freshness of its air. There were offices behind glass doors opposite, one with a pool of busy typists at work, the other seemingly empty. Lucinda picked up a glossy magazine, more as a prop than anything, to distract Gregg from talking. She badly needed to clear her head, if only to draw a line under what had happened that day thus far. A stream of soldiers passed while they were waiting on Alexander to reappear. Lucinda took to studying their badges. There were Turkish soldiers, Americans. Soon they learned that there was a twenty-five nation peace-keeping force in place, which would remain till the area became more stable. This was turning into something much more serious than she'd thought.

They entered Alexander's office, and he continued the no holds barred 'pep talk', intended to shock them into changing their plans to travel to the capital, Sukhumi. Gregg had raved about the place to Lucinda, which he'd described as one of the most beautiful coastal resorts in the world: a place where Gorbachev holidayed in his dacha; where ambassadors, kings and politicians partied in their spare time along it's coastline.

"Now I'm not going to beat around the bush," pacing. His uniform was baggy, and he looked pale, sweaty and forlorn. "This whole Galli region is extremely unstable. It is my duty to inform you that there is a very high risk of you both being taken hostage."

Lucinda glanced at Gregg side-ways, trying to read his body language, but if he was worried, he certainly didn't show it, sitting child-like, with his legs swinging over his hands.

"Seventy people have been taken from this immediate area. Not to mention over a hundred murders in the last year alone."

The Major's boots squeaked as he turned sharply, but inevitably his voice droned on. Of course, there was more. Much more bad news to lay on them, in the hope they'd scrap their plans. His voice continued, though more distant over time, as the clickety-clack of typists took over next door. Alexander carried a short wooden baton under his arm, which he clasped from time to time.

"Tragedy struck very close to home for us last week, Nothing left of him. Just a pile of prawns."

"That's terrible." Lucinda leaned forwards with a genuine look of concern.

Then, out of the poignant silence, came shockingly loud peels of laughter. He was holding onto his sides, as the Major stared back in horror, unsure how to react.

Lucinda suddenly 'got it'. Gregg had used this tactic many times, but possibly this had the best effect, as it completely knocked the Major off his stride. He looked to Lucinda for some explanation. Even the typewriters fell silent across the hall.

One of the women shattered the silence. "Why does he laugh at this terrible news?"

Lucinda merely shrugged. "Why don't you ask him yourself?"

Alexander promptly left the room, and the typing resumed, with Gregg staring into space, no doubt hatching yet another plan. Lucinda returned to her magazine, and the meaningless glossy ads.

A short time later a young woman called Angela appeared. She was in her early twenties, a very tall, leggy young blonde, by the Major, and wasn't about to muck around.

"I live in Sukhumi, but I work here, as part of a team that patrols the area. May I move you just for a second? My flak-jacket and helmet are under your chair, and I need to step outside for a second."

Lucinda and Gregg exchanged fleeting looks, with a shared expression that said it all.

"Don't worry. Regular issue," added stony-faced Angela, wriggling into the combat gear as if it was Saturday night, and she was breaking in a new pair of jeans.

It seemed wrong to be deploying such young women, if the area really was as dangerous as they were being led to believe.

The Major had certainly set the scene, and later that night, after his Russian housekeeper had prepared them a meal, he ramped up the action by bouncing them down the street in his jeep on a tour of charred, burned-out houses that had recently been 'ethnically cleansed'.

Once back in the relative safe comfort of the security headquarters, the Major finally thrashed out a deal. "Now you can ignore my advice if you want, but the way I see it, is that you have two options. First, is that you return to the relative security of the safety zone at Zugdidi. Or you can make your way onto Sukhumi, which is very unstable." He was pacing again. Back in control, with a pompous arrogant nose in the air. "Information is power, so I must inform you both that the main road to Sukhumi, the M64, is laden with unexploded landmines," he added matter-of-factly, almost running out of breath. "What time does your bus leave in the morning?"

"Eleven-thirty," they chorused.

Gregg met Lucinda with a powerful gaze. Despite worry lines shaping his forehead, he bubbled with a strange excitement. "So, what do you want to do, kid? It's entirely up to you."

"We're going to Sukhumi."

"There. The lady's decided."

There should have been a burst of applause. Instead, the whole building fell silent. The Major returned a defeated man, with the necessary papers to sign with details of their next-of-kin. "It's just a formality," he kindly reassured them, noticing Lucinda's eyes widen. "Just in case you might, erm, fall ill during your visit."

Lucinda was first to scribble her father's name in silence, imagining him receiving the terrible news that she'd been killed, blown up by a landmine, so far from home, and seemingly without cause. Perhaps freedom really had come at a high price, because for a second she again felt unrelated to any of her living relatives, so why the hell not?

Her second thought, as attention turned to Gregg, was if they did hit a landmine, would you even hear the explosion, or

43

would it be lights out? All over red rover, as her father would say. In recognition, a wave of parental pride suddenly washed over her, and she felt she had his blessing. Moreover, his stamp of approval, as he'd answered her Red Cross message saying he'd been following their travels on his map.

CHAPTER FIVE

PART TWO:

TICKING BOMB ON THE ROAD TO SUKHUMI

Angela seemed moody, near sulking when she met them at the bus stop the next morning as planned. She kept muttering under her breath that it was supposed to be her day off, much of which she should have been spending with her mother. She wore patched double denim, with her long blonde hair tied back in a straggly ponytail and refused to set her heavy bag down till the rusty old yellow bus arrived.

A crowd appeared out of nowhere, and suddenly they were elbow jostling with the determined rabble in a rush to get on and bag the best seats first. Lucinda and Gregg were sadly separated, though he clearly didn't seem to mind as much as her, since he wasn't wedged near the backseat with stony faced Angela, who barely spoke a word throughout the journey.

Gregg was wedged between a bunch of women traders at the front. "Hey Lucinda. These women think we should be married. What do you think?"

"I think you should sit down." She answered powerfully, feeling her cheeks flush as the front row turned and giggled back at her.

Lucinda sought solace by pressing her face against the hot glass and her fearful reflection, but she could hear the Major's voice clearly as the bus sped on.

"Partisan soldiers have been pulling loose landmines out of the River Inguri for weeks now. I fear it's only a matter of time before a bus load of civilians are blown up and killed."

Lucinda was trapped. There was nothing she could do to stop the bus now, in the middle of the motorway. Resigned to her fate, she reflected on how this was the most hideously unheroic debacle to be amongst when contemplating losing your life. The noises and smells were intolerable, squashed against flabby armed women wrestling to hold down squealing pigs in the aisles, and with strangle-holds on near frantic hens roughly tied in sacks as they cruelly, endlessly, sped along.

She truly wanted to stand up and scream out "Quick. Get off. This bus is about to blow." But that would have been disrespectful to everyone on board including Angela, who sat, sphinx-like, never moving a muscle throughout the journey. Small talk was completely off limits, as was panicking like a spoilt child. Instead, Lucinda slipped down in her seat and decided to take in the sights, for her eyes were unaccustomed to the horrors of civil war, where civilians, not soldiers, family pets, and much-loved heirlooms were caught in the crossfire. Their charred remains scattered across acres of scorched ground like the surface of the moon.

During their journey up the M64, they were at times forced to take detours off road, around bridges that had been blown up and destroyed. It was during those moments, as the giant rubber tyres zig-zagged onto the grass verge, that Lucinda's heart leapt into her mouth. Gregg roared things like "Nearly there now," but his deep and normally reassuring voice had raised an octave.

'Finally Sukhumi twinkled before them lush and green, with it's wide avenues Italian architecture, and tall gum trees.' They had made it. They had defied the Major's warning. But what of their return journey, and of the others on the coach who faced this danger daily? To walk in their shoes was a humbling experience, and one that changed Lucinda for life.

CHAPTER FIVE

PART THREE:

NEVER TURN YOUR BACK ON THE SUN

Having merely served her duty, Angela sourly bade them fare-well at the flat they would be renting. It belonged to one of the young English teachers at the local school. Since the Georgian invasion, three generations of her family had taken refuge in their summer mountain home, where the air was sweeter, fresh-er and still, and where they could escape from the angry swarms of mosquitoes that raided the market close-by.

"Please follow me, I'd like to show you around."

Lucinda was instantly drawn to the young teacher, who was stylishly presented and accomplished for her years. The wood-en bungalow was charming. There was the throb of a frog cho-rus right outside the window, and a pleasant wooden veranda Lucinda had ear-marked for sitting under the stars with Gregg, sipping wine.

"Oh, it's perfect," she sighed, loosening her scarf and allow-ing herself to breathe naturally for the first time since their ter-rifying bus ride.

"Tell me please. Why have you come to my country?"

"We want to help if we can," Gregg, who'd thus far been si-lent, piped up . "Lucinda and I want to try and set up a student exchange programme with some of your pupils here in Sukhumi. We know you are twin towns with Kilmarnock in Scotland. Lucinda's Scottish, so it's something close to her heart."

Lucinda felt her cheeks flush shyly, and yet she had no choice but to go along with the latest yarn. Worse still, she watched Kama's big brown eyes fill with tears that finally spilled over, streaking her pale cheeks with black rivers of mascara. She in-stinctively grabbed Lucinda's hand and stroked it.

"That's wonderful. Thank you. Are you a teacher too?"

"Well, no. Not exactly. I work on a newspaper."

"Ah, you're a journalist. That makes sense. No foreign civilians are allowed into our country now. Not since the Georgian invasion. I cried, my grandmother cried, when tanks rolled into Sukhumi. We watched our beautiful city burn from our home in the mountains. It fills me with hope, you know, that good people like you have taken the trouble to visit us and speak on our behalf. The rest of the world must know of the genocide that's taken place here. Many hundreds of Abkhazians have been killed. Many have lost their homes. People are scared, many starving. We're trapped here, at the mercy of soldiers who shoot around our bedroom windows for fun. Their president comes on our television daily, telling us we'll all soon be killed. That they're coming to get us. They play with our minds."

Kama's outburst was not only shocking but alarming they were up to their necks in it. She left looking pale and exhausted but promised to return in a couple of days, with a cheeky wink aimed at Lucinda just as she was leaving.

"Why did you say that?" she hissed like a cat with its hackles raised, as soon as the door closed. Gregg, the well-practised punch-bag, braced, and met her with the angelic expression of a choir boy.

"What? I swear I didn't do anything wrong. I will genuinely make enquiries as soon as we get back home."

"What's the point? People like Kama can't travel. They're living in a state unrecognised by the rest of the world. They will most likely all be killed soon. Not to mention us, if we hang around much longer."

"Lucinda, calm down. We've only just arrived, and yes, life is tough here, but the locals like Kama are survivors. Theirs is a worthy cause. They're fighting for freedom."

The heat inside the wooden bungalow was stifling, so they drifted outside to join the loud hum of frogs and watch a neighbouring tower block light up in coloured sequence. Other than that, there was silence, only dotted with sporadic Kalashnikov fire lighting the horizon in the distance.

"Tomorrow we'll go to the market and stock up on supplies."

"Isn't that hugely risky with counterfeit money?"

"We'll just go and suss things out. Lucinda, babe, you've got to trust me."

Darkness quickly closed around them, and she fell fast asleep before making it to bed. Gregg covered her gently with a heavy coat and slept sporadically on the wicker chair beside her. Finally, the sand road in front of them lit up red as the sun rose steadily through a heat haze.

The sound of children playing nearby settled Lucinda as she washed in cold water and got herself dressed for the day. The mirror opposite their bed confirmed she was covered in an angry mosaic of mosquito bites. She wore a scarf and did her best to hide them, but they were already raised and itchy. Gregg was busily arranging the dollars they would take, leaving with single-dollar socks and a whole bunch of filthy money carefully stashed in his underwear.

"Now stay close to me," he warned as they were leaving. "Don't flash any of this money around until I say so, OK?"

"OK," she nodded dumbly, now used to being on exercise.

Cutting through a run-down area of tenement buildings, they could have been anywhere in the world, save for the beautiful iron sculptures and bus shelters fashioned out of seashells, making them stand out as works of art as the promenade merged with the market.

Lucinda matched Gregg stride for stride, and from the fringes, the noise and intoxicating smells made it clear that the market was already buzzing. There were groups furiously haggling over nothing. Poor caged animals fighting for their lives, and the bronzed, toothy older set hastily seeking shade on wooden benches under sunsplashed trees.

Having successfully passed off a couple of dollars without any ugly repercussions, they became bolder, and haggled over the price of meat and fish, becoming regulars to the marketplace. In days, they were on nodding terms with several stallholders, who viewed the pair not only as foreign oddities, but also walking wallets.

"Look ... Look, see!" came the shouts, as soon as they entered the confines of the gates. Gathering in swarms, they tried to sell them U.N ration packs they'd somehow gotten hold of, and although it became clear they wouldn't be starving, Lucinda felt waves of guilt every time they spread their counterfeit money around those poor peasant folk.

It also became clear that they'd need to re-organise their sleeping arrangements although the main bedroom was characterful and very beautiful, with its dark mahogany furniture and classical paintings, it was full of mosquitoes, with their menacing drone, dusk 'til dawn. Gregg suggested they move to the cooler living room, where they could set up camp under the dining table.

"There, you'll get a better sleep tonight Lucinda, and if soldiers do shoot around our windows again, we'll barely hear it." He spread out the green silk eiderdown on the floor over their pillows, and they settled outside on the veranda until the sun bobbled and slipped below the horizon.

Lucinda slept soundly, and only woke when she heard noises coming from the kitchen. Gregg wanted to make the morning special, so he had boiled a couple of eggs for breakfast, and as they settled back on the floor to enjoy them, the front door burst open, and sunlight streamed across the floor.

Ludmilla, one of Kama's colleagues from the local schoolappeared, and without explanation began a tour of the house and its contents with a rather bemused older couple on tow. Their expression said it all, and after a whistle-stop tour the door slammed and they were gone. It was only after Kama paid them a visit later that morning that they finally learned the truth. Gregg was shaving in the bathroom, so Lucinda answered the door.

"My God, Lucinda. Look at you. What has happened? You look terrible. Have you been drinking?" Lucinda smiled ruefully, and loosened her sleeve, revealing an angry map of mosquito bites. "Oi, this is terrible. You must leave at once. Come to my summerhouse and meet with my family. I've told my grandmother all about you, and she would love to meet you both."

"Ludmilla burst in early this morning and showed a couple of strangers around unannounced," Lucinda blurted out.

"Yes, I'm sorry about that. The owner of this house needs to sell quickly. The furniture is also up for sale. Clearly someone should have told you. I'm so sorry."

Her stylish, over pronounced pout said it all. Most Abkhazian's had the luxury of a second home, and most, it seemed, were tucked away in the mountains, where they would retreat to in summer when the weather got extremely hot and humid.

Kama turned to leave, with her trademark wink aimed in Lucinda's direction. "My sister. I'll see you later. My brother will pick you up here at six o'clock. Oh, and please be ready. He really hates to be kept waiting!" The door slammed, and she was gone. She could have been a great actress with her theatrical entrances and exits. A flash of ankle, a flick of billowing scarf; her glamorous expressions seemed legendary.

"You stay here, babe, and get ready. I'll go to the market on my own today."

"No, it's too dangerous. I'm coming with you."

"Look, Lucinda, the most dangerous thing about the market at this time of day are the swarms of mosquitoes that clearly find you as tasty as I do!"

"Well okay, but don't take all day. I'll be waiting out on the veranda."

She waved to Gregg 'til he'd disappeared out of sight on the sandy dirt road that led directly into town. An hour passed happily, with Lucinda changing and trying to look her very best for Kama's family. She did her best to mix and match from a few meagre items buried in her dishevelled rucksack. Clearly, wherever she was, old habits die hard. She eventually settled outside to watch her neighbour's children playing, giant pigs lumbering right alongside, and the odd motorbike which stopped her from snoozing.

Finally, she saw Gregg's tall figure returning in the distance. Her heart skipped a beat. He still had her in the palm of his hands. He looked laden down, and held up one of the bags as he got within earshot.

"Hey Lucinda, I've brought you a present which I think you'll like."

A loud crack sounded in the distance, followed by rapid rounds of Kalashnikov fire. Lucinda stood up. As the putrid smoke cleared from misty grey to toxic yellow Gregg crumpled head-first onto the road, shopping spilling all around him.

"Oh my God Oh my God, no" She cried, a terrified scream the most otherworldly of sounds. Gregg lifted his head and quietly called out to her.

"It's okay Lucinda. They just got me in the buttocks. Just remember I was the one who made you laugh."

He fell flat again, and this time he never roused. People ran out of their apartments. The women quickly gathered their children inside. The local men formed a posse and stood in a sombre circle around Gregg.

The next thing Lucinda could remember was meeting with Alexander, who appeared at her bedside. Instead of looking vindicated, he seemed sadder and more tired than ever. More grey, more baggy eyed and forlorn.

"I'm going home on a fortnight's leave. If you wish, I'll gladly accompany you home."

CHAPTER SIX

NEVER MISS YOUR FATHER'S FUNERAL

Returning home to a grey rain-soaked England in the grip of a thunderstorm seemed fitting. It was October, the cold just beginning to bite. The aeroplane wings nearly touched down in sequence before the landing gear grudgingly arrived.

Alexander peered down at the familiar scene with a practised smugness as they glided down over the white hangars splitting grey and green. He'd completed his tour of duty by returning her safely, but to what? He neither knew nor cared, though in true military style he debriefed her in an airport security office, and arranged for her to travel on with yet another officer returning north on leave.

"I can manage from here on my own," she protested, but Alexander would hear none of it.

"You've been through a terrible trauma, and are most probably suffering from shock. Believe me, I've seen battlehardened soldiers break over less." Stamping hard on his cigarette to punctuate the fact, he left with a firm handshake, and as usual some final words of wisdom. "Good luck, Lucinda. Just remember, wherever your travels take you in life, you are the product of all your experiences. I'm sure your family are all very proud."

Funny, but up until that point, she hadn't given her family too much thought, other than hoping she hadn't upset them too much by being absent from their lives for the best part of two years. During that period, she only been allowed to send a couple of Red Cross letters to her father, which had been vetted in Moscow then Geneva, and had received one reply, saying he'd been following her journey on his old, battered map. It came as a shock to her, that their relationship still existed, as her prolonged absence must've caused him unimaginable pain at the loneliest of times. None of her family had travelled much before, and had never expressed the need to, and yet she had been a restless spirit from the beginning, making her the oddball. Journeying north finally freed her from her chaperone, and she could breathe at last. The wide, sweeping greenery and the train's rattling motion helped to gradually ease her pain. She would ring her father when she got a bit closer to home. No need to make him restless, though she could already imagine his twinkling blue eyes through a crushing embrace. She wouldn't close hers, not just yet; she feared seeing Gregg. Still in shock, she was suffering from tremors, and bouts of uncontrollable shaking head to toe. Fortunately, she was alone in the carriage, and could stretch out. A double rainbow caught her eye in the distance. Surely a lucky sign. She smiled, as the train split the countryside in half under darkening skies.

Installed in a neighbouring town's B & B, Lucinda finally made the call home. She'd gauge her father's reaction before she told all. There was so much to tell she didn't know where to begin, or how much of it he might tolerate. Standing in the hallway of her host's house, the phone rang out shrilly. She let it ring for a while, before curiously setting it down.

The same thing happened at various times over the next couple of days, and Lucinda began feeling more anxious. With his health failing, her father rarely ventured far. She decided she'd ring her cousin instead, trying a different approach. This time a voice answered right away. Lucinda tried to sound casually upbeat.

"Well, hello stranger. It's Lucinda."

"I know. You're back then?" The voice was abrupt.

"How is my favourite aunt?"

"She's surviving. Though she gets very upset when I mention your name. Look, has all your travelling stopped? I'm quite prepared to send you a couple of thousand pounds, if you are willing to stay home and face up to your responsibilities."

The conversation fell silent.

"What?" Lucinda finally uttered, feeling a ball of anger stir in the pit of her stomach. She wanted to hang up, but she couldn't bring herself to do it. Her cousin was rattling on without listening as usual, but one sentence got her attention.

"Would you like the good or the bad news? Your father died several months ago. There was a good turn out at the local church. Oh, and my friend Jeanette's gone and got herself engaged." She let out a blood-curdling scream of her excitement. "Can you believe it?"

Lucinda dropped the receiver flat. "Oh, fuck off you stupid woman."

She staggered from the hallway all the way upstairs to her room, sobbing as she reached the doorway. Feeling like her chest had been ripped open again, she slumped down on the edge of her bed.

CHAPTER SIX

PART TWO:

NEVER GO UPSTAIRS
WHEN THERE'S A HAUNTING

With barely a wink of sleep, Lucinda began the long drive home, unsure of what she'd find there. It was a starting point, nothing more. Feeling the bottom had dropped out of her world, and clutching the key to her family home, she had to make several detours and stops because of her shaking, and it felt like the longest, loneliest drive of her life, despite lights twinkling through lashing rain in the distance.

Navigating the loch-side's narrow and winding road took some getting used to, but she knew every twist and turn like the back of her hand, unlike the horror she was facing. Pulling up on the opposite kerb, she glanced up at her old bedroom window. The house looked bleak, newly abandoned, but something else more pressing caught her attention as soon as she pushed open the car door. There was a gushing sound of water, like a waterfall coming from the house.

Lucinda slammed her door and ran across the road. The noise was getting louder. She tried her key. It opened, and with it a torrent of water gushed out. The house was flooded, with multiple burst pipes. She waded knee deep into the living room. Family photos and much-loved ornaments floated past her in swirling patterns. Oddly, the sound of the phone ringing in the hallway came as a welcome relief.

"Ah, Lucinda. Is that you?"

"Yes, of course," she snapped back angrily. "I just can't believe my eyes, that's all. Have you any clue what I've come back to? The place is flooded. There are multiple burst pipes, and the ceilings are about to come down."

"Ah, of course you wouldn't know, would you? What with being away for so long." Her cousin had a knack of riling her up, but this time she'd gone too far.

"Know what?"

"Well, we've had the coldest temperatures this winter for several hundred years. It's been minus fifteen for weeks. Haven't you at least read about it, or seen the news?"

She couldn't risk another obscenity, in the case this time she heard her. Still thinking with a military mind, which had rubbed off from Alexander, she realised it was in her own interest to keep lines of communication open, as her father had made her cousin chief executor of his will in her absence. She took a deep breath and perched on the telephone table, spanning a bridge over the gurgling water.

"I'll get on to the insurers."

"Is it habitable?"

"Definitely not. I'll call you when I'm settled."

So many thoughts raced through Lucinda's mind; flashbacks of her childhood, her moody teenage years, and her wedding to Mike. It had been such a happy home, spanning decades and filled with their positive energy. Now, the place was just a gaping black hole on the edge of extinction. Lucinda felt her parents at every turn. She had the oddest sense, that either of them might be about to make an unwelcome appearance and start demanding explanations.

It was turning dark outside, and she was much too afraid to hang around, especially without electricity. Lucinda decided to lock the house of horrors back up and run for her life.

Safely installed in a hotel across the road, she was back in touch with her cousin, and the insurer's loss adjuster, who'd be paying a visit to assess the damage. Meantime, he instructed her to keep the home fires burning by topping the fire up with coal.

"If you keep it burning day and night," he added, "we may just save the wooden floors."

It felt such a cruel time to have this newly afflicted burden, without the time and energy to properly grieve for Gregg, and yet she became militarised in her effort. Lucinda ordered a sandwich and coffee and pencilled herself a rota. She'd stoke the fire three times daily: morning, noon and night. It was the night drops she feared the most, as the house was now eerily dank and quiet. Like a wreck lying at the bottom of the ocean, it creaked and groaned in all the wrong places.

The night runs near midnight proved the hardest. She only hoped no one was watching, as her car would career into the driveway, disturbing the gravel path. She'd leap out just inches from the front door and, angling her torch, would lift the hod of coal, run into the pitch-dark living room, and literally throw the coal in the direction of the embers, causing a great roar like Hades galloping back from hell. It was literally over in seconds. She was terrified to look over her shoulder in case she saw anything she'd regret. This went on for three days and nights, and Lucinda was on the verge of collapsing with exhaustion.

On night four, as she bent to pick up the hod of coal, her worst fears were realised. She heard a ghostly, high-pitched moan coming from one of the upstairs bedrooms. Her heart was beating ten to the dozen as she prised open the front door.

"Oh, I knew this would happen. I can't do this" she whimpered. After a few steadying breaths, "Come on Lucinda. Get a grip," she rallied, but the wailing got louder as she stepped inside. She had no option but to go upstairs, which went against the grain when facing a haunting. She relished these horrors in her teens, but now she was all grown up and part of the action.

The unearthly furor was coming from her parent's bedroom. "God help me!" she shouted, and ran inside, flashing her torch around like a weapon. Still nothing. She pinned the wailing down to within their bedroom cupboard, which she gingerly opened and peered inside. Steam was rising from the boiler, which had set the smoke alarm off, which in turn had almost run out of battery over time; thus the wailing like a banshee!

CHAPTER SEVEN

NEVER TRUST A LOVED ONE'S OPINION

The days drifted into weeks that ran into months, with Lucinda adrift at her family home pondering her future. Her cousin tried to get her to see reason and stay where she was, finally 'facing up to her responsibilities,' and in waded Mike's voice from time to time. "You know you're a lucky woman Lucinda. One day you'll be a very rich woman. If I go first, you'll be able to sell this house, not to mention the money you'll get from your mother and father's."

"Oh, yeah, Mike. Just listen to yourself. I'll be a rich old woman, and all the people I love on this earth will be gone, but I'll be loaded!"

The loves of her life couldn't have been more different. Gregg would be encouraging her to take wings and fly. She was desperately searching her soul for answers, looking for clues, listening for that one definitive voice.

One day she was leafing through Gregg's old horoscopes, and the pages fell open to the day he was shot. She read the shocking entry, holding her breath.

"Scorpio. November 6th. 'You said goodbye to the sun today. Be yourself. Lock your spine and walk tall. Never listen to those who doubt your talents." Gregg's unmistakable, deep voice cut through loud and clear. Not only that, but the room filled with his scent. It was so shocking that she jumped up and slammed the door. "You're talented Lucinda. You should use it. If I had the gift of music and writing like you, I'd be off to America. It's the land of opportunity. It recognises talent, believe me. I've read your diary and can't count the times I've tried to describe my stay in Poti, but you, you had it in a nutshell. 'We strayed most nights along the reedy banks and gravelly inlets of the river Rioni, and like Poti itself it looked moody, purple and black against the setting sun.'"

Of course, Gregg was right as usual, whether he was inside her head or standing in front of her. She felt torn leaving what was left of her family a second time, but she had no fight left in her conscience.

The next time she spoke to her cousin it was with the family house repaired, cleared and sold, and with the determined air to begin a new chapter. She had packed all her diaries and a few items of clothing inside a small rucksack, along with a collection of maps, and a claret and blue leaflet with a timetable, encouraging one and all to "GO GREYHOUND!"

There was suddenly a backrush of excitement, the way she once felt with Gregg on the eve of one of their travels, and she could barely contain her excitement as she stared down the phone, hearing her cousin's voice like some cruel interruption.

"Hi, it's me, Lucinda."

"I know. Where are you? Mother's been asking."

"Oh, just some hotel. I'm leaving in the morning. I'm going to America."

A familiar, earth-shatteringly long silence followed, as Lucinda looked around the dated trinkets in the hotel lobby.

"What for? Why would you want to go there?"

"I've been keeping a diary all the time I've been away. It's become, well, more than a hobby. It's a passion. Something I really enjoy. I can't explain it, but the words just flow out of me. I must see if I can make it work."

"I see."

"Can I at least say goodbye to my aunt?"

"I don't think that would be a wise idea. She's very upset. Anyway, goodbye. I don't suppose we'll be seeing you again."

What? No, wait. "We're talking America, not the ends of the earth."

Her cousin had slammed the phone down. It was seminal. The pivotal 'go it alone' moment. Their final conversation.

CHAPTER SEVEN

PART TWO:

NEVER PACK A PEN-KNIFE

Lucinda was fit to burst as she and her best friend Ellery boarded their plane to Boston. Ellery would be visiting her sister, but at least they could share the long flight together.

"My God, Lucinda, what have you packed into this little rucksack?"

"Oh, just some essentials, and the hardcopy of my book." She dropped it in lightly, and then waited for the explosion.

"Your book. My goodness. It weighs a ton. What exactly are those 'essentials'?"

They were strapping in for the long haul, ignoring the flight attendant's instructions around the blowing of the tiny whistle.

"Oh, just my mosquito net and Swiss army knife. Some first-aid and medicine."

"You've changed, girl. You're not the Lucinda I remember, with her keen fashion sense, high heels and jewellery. More like 'Jane of the Jungle'!"

They giggled together on the bumpy take-off, and for once Lucinda didn't mind her bum hanging in the air, or the wings teasing sunlight into the cabin. She was finally going to make something of her life. Her destiny was in her own hands for the first time ever, and what's more, to hell with loneliness. She relished the challenge and believed every word Gregg had told her after reading her book, cover to cover.

"This is great Lucinda. You'll have no difficulty finding a publisher for your work. America's the place. They'll snap your hand off. There are more little independent publishers there than anywhere else on the planet. They'll want to interview you on all the local radio stations. It'll be 'small town' at first, but greater things will happen. It's all mapped out for you. All you got to do is go and grab it!"

They were soon doing a 'cheers' with fizzy prosecco. Ellery to being reunited with her eldest sister again, and Lucinda to being the girl that fell out of the family tree who finally found herself. Several plastic bottles later, and Ellery was snoring loudly, her cheek flushed and pressed hard against their window.

"Is she okay?" the annoyed voice of their rather aged flight attendant cut in.

"Oh, yes thanks. She's just a little tired."

"We all are, honey."

How rude, Lucinda thought, drifting off, and happily leaving the muffled hubbub behind her. There was an aggressive edge to that woman that Lucinda would soon see was common in America.

Boston Airport was where they hugged and said their goodbyes.

"Look after yourself, Lucinda. Don't talk to strangers!"

"Oh no? Fat chance. There will be plenty of those around!"

"Aren't you scared of being alone though?" Ellery's voice echoed around the marble hallway.

Soon she was lost amid bobbing hats and bodies, all rushing to meet different schedules.

"Can I have a white coffee, please?" Lucinda asked kindly.

"Coffee's black honey, or are you blind?"

She was clearly going to stand out from the crowd from then on, like it or not, and there was more heckling as she tried to buy her ticket through to the capital from an automated ticket machine.

"Well hurry up Miss. Don't just stand there staring at it. Get your dollars in. I've a connection to catch." Clearly this was going to be more difficult than she thought, though fame was just teasing from around the corner.

CHAPTER SEVEN

PART THREE:

NEVER LET A COUNTRY SWALLOW YOU WHOLE

It soon became clear to Lucinda that she needed a hire car just to get around, as travelling anywhere in America was exhausting, with the constant suck and surge of determined bodies intent on getting around. Even crossing the capital's wide streets became something of a challenge, which nearly made Lucinda grab stranger's hands just to make it to the other side when the racing track signs winked green.

She had careened through Maine, Rhode Island, and Boston, and took a sidestep on the Greyhound into Tennessee, just to see what Nashville was really like. Waiting in the draughty Greyhound depot, she queued without spotting a single Stetson, though once on the coach the tall, silver-haired driver didn't disappoint; he called out their destination stops partly in song.

"All off the coach for Chattanooga ...Let's Go Greyhound for Chattanooga, everyone!"

It was only when Lucinda reached the relatively rolling green heartlands of North and South Carolina that she could finally relax and breathe. She checked herself into the Red Roof Inn and approached a man on reception.

"Hi, I've just arrived and would like to hire a car."

"You from England, miss? Gee, that's really awesome. Ma'am, may I take a look at your passport?"

"Yes, sure." The guy scratched through his greasy hair for an eternity, while he ogled between Lucinda's passport photo and her. She brought him quickly back down to earth. "May I hire a car or not?"

"Oh, for sure you can. Just as long as you return it to Washington. That's where it'll be coming from." Before Lucinda got the chance to reply, the skinny guy was cranking up the phone. "Hank, I got a woman here, she's from England, goddamn. I'm speaking on her behalf, cause she don't speak good English." he gave a cheeky wink across the desk, as though he'd done her a favour. "You ready, miss? Here, you speak to him."

"It's quite alright, I've changed my mind."

"As you wish, ma'am. Here's your room key. Have a good one."

He dropped the key from a height into her hand, and she was finally able to escape and lie down. Lucinda began spreading out her state map as soon as she'd recovered. It seemed she had no option but to stay on the Greyhound bus and move further south into Georgia. It struck her then, that she had made a few contacts when she'd travelled through Georgia, its namesake in Russia. Her diary confirmed her hunch. The American delegate's name was Carlton Parker, and better yet, she had his full address, from state down to zip code.

"Bingo," she muttered under her breath. "He did say if I was ever in Atlanta to look him up. He's bound to be well-connected with the likes of publishers. I can feel Gregg's opportunism about to rub off."

Despite being relatively wealthy since the sale of her parent's house, Lucinda was keen to spend what she had carefully, leading her to check into a rather run-down hotel on the seedier side of town. It felt good to lock the door behind her, and to turn on her ancient television set. Just as she did, there was a huge clap of thunder, followed by neon pink lightning, which hit the outside of the building, leaving the hotel sign hanging by a thread.

"Just as I say, Jim. There has been a severe hurricane warning issued for the city of Atlanta. It's certain to damage many homes. People are being advised to get out of town."

The voice trailed off, overshadowed by the slamming of car doors right outside her tall bay window, and the clickety-clack of high heels frantically tearing along the pavements. It all made sense along with the commentary.

Lucinda peered behind the filthy red velvet curtain. Sure enough, people were running for their lives, but for her there was no point. She had nowhere to run to, so she would have to hunker down and ride out the storm. However, she had been fascinated by the locals' reactions. They'd clearly been through it many times before and had a healthy respect for the wind and weather, which blew in as quickly as she had.

The hotel may have been rickety, but the walls were thick and strong, and empty streets that had been hastily deserted soon rallied to the sound of chatter and car doors slamming in sequence. This time there was laughter as groups regaled their own personal stories, of the frightening night that was. Lucinda decided to ring Carlton Parker the next morning, and as promised she was standing in the draughty hall, trapped under the sleazy gaze of the lanky man on reception.

"Hello, is that Carlton Parker?"

"For sure. Who's this?"

"Well, I don't suppose you'll remember me, but we met as part of a delegation that came to Poti, Georgia right at the end of last year. My name's Lucinda Grey. I'm a Scottish journalist. You did say, if I was ever in Atlanta, to be sure and look you up."

"I did. Yeah, I remember you now. How nice to connect with you. May I be of assistance while you're staying in my town?"

"Well, as a matter of fact, I've written a novel, and am looking for a publisher who might be interested."

"I see, that's exciting stuff. Leave it with me, and I'll send some feelers out."

"How kind. Thank you so much."

"Let me take down your details. You're staying where?" There was a sharp intake of breath at the other side. "You better pack your bags quickly. I'll come and pick you up immediately. Now, don't be scared, but I must tell you, that you are staying in a very run-down and dangerous part of town. It's renowned for violence, and many murders. I'll book you into a hotel in La Grange, right near my residence."

"Oh, thank you, but no. I'm quite happy staying where I am for now."

There was another pause. Carlton was clearly puzzled. He mixed in higher circles, and she was rubbing shoulders with the bums and down-and-outs. He probably assumed she was better than that. Still, true to his word, Lucinda was soon in touch with a publisher, who was more interested in her Scottish accent than he seemed in her work.

"Say that again, you sound awesome. So, you'd best send over a hard copy to my office. We'll get back to you within the month."

The receiver dropped, as did her mood. This was clearly going to drag on a while. There'd be no immediate pot of gold, and little chance of any rainbow, and she was in limbo again, her life on hold, while totally putting her faith in others. She'd wake every morning to the mailman banging on doors all along the corridor, but hers didn't rattle 'til the month was nearly over, and she ripped open the brown envelope with trembling fingers. There was a short appraisal in spidery writing, though she had to read it several times over, to make sense of the shocking revelation.

In three remarks he'd shredded her dreams, cut her down to size with just these three little phrases she repeated over and over. "Over-bug rambling with a child-like naivety, therefore, not something that would interest us."

Lucinda's tears splashed onto the page until it looked like blotting paper.

"What now? What's to become of me? Gregg, you bastard! You made me believe in this piece of work. Why Gregg? Why? Why did you have to lie?"

Lucinda locked herself away for several weeks, until an ad in a newspaper grabbed her attention. "Miami to Paris, special one-time offer. Single flight £63."

"Paris," she beamed, repeating it out loud. Little cobbled streets, rain splashing her ankles. Without explanation, she simply had to go. America had taken her by storm, but she simply wasn't ready, nor was her writing. She was, however, ready to find her very own new home.

Within a week, she was queuing in the Greyhound office to check her luggage into the underfloor hold. Lucinda slept most of the journey down to Florida, and when she woke, it was to a perfect beach scene, straight out of the glossy mags. There were groups of guys walking around clutching surfboards. Nearly everyone was walking the palm-tree-lined beach promenade in tropical swimwear. Sunglasses were de rigueur. All very uniform, yet clearly relaxed.

"Okay," yelled the driver. "All passengers for Miami, be prepared to leave the coach."

As she queued behind the black bobbing heads, Lucinda could see her French aeroplane on the tarmac over the wall. "My God," she muttered, "I'm going to be tight for time."

Clutching her baggage tags, she joined another queue, and when finally at the front learned the awful truth.

"Your bags were loaded on the coach that travelled before us. Join the end of that one over there," said the handler casually, as if she had all the time in the world.

"Excuse me," she beamed, holding out her tag, while quietly sashaying to the head of the next queue. "May I just take my bag and go. My plane is about to leave. It's the brown suitcase right here."

"Get to the back of the queue, honey. You gotta wait your turn like everybody else."

"You don't understand. I will miss my flight to Paris. Now give me my bag, and I will leave you alone." It was hot, and tempers were fraying. Hot diesel fumes were metallic in her mouth. "Look, just pass me my bag, and I'll be gone."

"You isn't going nowhere little lady. I'm going to make sure of that."

The baggage handler had a pretentious uniform, considering the nature of her job. She looked more like a police officer in her blue striped tunic, with a shiny badge on her hat.

"This woman is a racist. You saw how she just spoke to me. Hang fire, cause I'm calling the cops."

Lucinda saw red and grabbed her by the shirt. Despite her size, she swung her off her feet. It certainly got the queue against her.

"She *is* a racist. That's a disgraceful way to act."

The tension was palpable. Lucinda walked to the other side of the tarmac, and sat there remorselessly cross-legged until she heard the Miami-Dade police car screech in in a wide arc.

The officer was tall, silver haired. She could see the baggage handler's over animated accusations, and knew if she kept quiet, she might plead innocence. Anything was worth a try. It would be a crime if she were to be arrested. He listened, scribbling in his notebook, and finally sauntered over.

"Now, what happened, ma'am, as you recall?"

"Well, my luggage was put on the coach before mine. This is my tag, but nobody told me, so I asked that lady if she would kindly give me my bag, so I could still catch my flight to Paris. Then she started calling me racist. I really don't know why."

"Uh-huh, yes. OK. I get it." He produced a Miami-Dade incident card out of his top pocket, and handed it down to Lucinda with a little wink.

"Are you arresting me?"

"Oh no, little lady, it's just a keepsake. Now step into the car. Mind your head."

"Thanks."

The other officer nodded and smiled. Then they sped off in silence, save for the flashing blue light's noisy siren.

Lucinda had sunk low into the comfy backseat, and was safely tucked away behind bullet proof glass as they sped into the airport. The officer got her straight through onto her flight without any fuss.

"Thank you so much," she gushed.

"Not at all little lady. The pleasure's been all mine."

He doffed his cap with a gentle bow, and she barely found her seat and sat down before the plane took off for Paris. It was a thrilling, movie-style, surreal exit, and a worthy way to end her American misadventure.

CHAPTER EIGHT

MORTALITY AND THE MENOPAUSE
(TEN YEARS LATER)

Returning to the U. K. via America and Paris, Lucinda was determined to work hard, play hard, and take a serious look at improving her life. Now in her mid-forties, she was a single woman, completely adrift without any family ties. She'd bought a house with what was left of her money and was writing between six and seven hours a day, having secured funding through the Scottish Arts Council. On the surface, everything was hunky-dory – then it struck. She became menopausal.

The symptoms had cruelly crept up on her, subtly, one by one. The tears, the tantrums; raking through her wardrobes and not knowing why; jumping in her car and ending up in obscure, far-flung lay-bys with no recollection of getting there. She'd upped her weekly calls to Ellery, who'd endure her sobbing on the other end of the line.

"You know, I think you should see a doctor."

"There's nothing wrong, really. I'm still missing Gregg, and have been crying for Scotland."

"More like Britain!"

"Sorry."

"Don't be. You helped me when I left William."

Really, the final straw came when she made a big pot of home-made chicken and rice soup and threw the lot over her sofa. Her writing ended abruptly when she found herself in a gynaecological ward in nothing but a flimsy paper gown, with a bird's eye view of consultant Doctor Wisdom poking around her privates while her ankles were thrust up on stirrups.

"It's clear," came the verdict from his backside, as he stood, furiously washing his hands at the sink in front. "You have a very large fibroid. Around ten centimetres in diameter."

The room blurred as he trotted out the symptoms she'd been experiencing for almost a year. Mood swings leading to irrational behaviour; facial flushing and crying over nothing; lower back pain and urinary tract infections. The list seemed endless. She ended up with an oophorectomy, of which even the preposterous name made her feel a laughingstock. Barely woman. Worse still, motherhood had simply passed her by, without being particularly maternal.

She linked it to an incident in her childhood, remembering her own mother talking over the high fence to her neighbour next door, asking about the woman two doors down. She hadn't been seen in her garden for months, having been struck by a mystery illness. It caused her mother to shake her head soberly, and whisper odd sentences like, 'everything's been taken away.' Lucinda just assumed she must have died, till one day her head poked through a billowing line of washing with a great big gappy smile!

It made her address her own mortality and place in the world, and still felt shocking that she was the last in line; the final link in the sordid chain that had separated her from her family, whom she'd rob of a lengthy legacy, as the tree would not only rot, but be uprooted after she died.

The theme continued well into her fifties, attending more funerals than weddings, around three to one. Though she'd make an appearance, she'd quietly leave before the service, as missing her own father's had left her badly scarred. Many were musicians she'd known while working alongside husband Mike. Seeing how many of the most handsome had aged was truly shocking. She wondered what they thought of her. Many had been alcoholics for decades; alcohol and music went hand in hand. She'd seen it destroy many lives of the world's most colourful characters.

Today, it was the turn of their former drummer, simply known to one and all as 'Jackie.' He had merited a particular send-off, as his trademark had always been his car, an ancient hearse he'd converted and painted in psychedelic colours to cheer the old Rolls Royce engine up. He'd bought it because of the long back and runners, which meant he could slide his whole drum kit in. The downside was he could be seen for miles and was easily targeted by local police.

"Okay Mister Foreman. Step out of the car." It was a familiar routine, so Jackie knew he had just enough time to make and smoke the thinnest of roll-ups.

The officers knelt and began examining his tyres. "Mister Foreman. Your offside right tyre is bald."

He playfully slapped his son Jackie Junior. "You stupid boy. You've put it back on inside out!"

"Ah, get away with you, Jackie!"

They'd always tear up the report roaring and laughing at his cheek, but even he, though his organs were well and truly pickled and preserved, succumbed to the unenviable task of returning to Mother Earth some thirty years early. Those revealing snapshots into Lucinda's prime made her more determined than ever to make a success of her life. She had seen so much, changed so much, and yet life was now speeding by full throttle. She would have to quit the dead-end jobs she'd been using to fund her writing ambition and live off her savings if she was ever going to make it.

CHAPTER NINE

NEVER GET UP TO YOUR NECK IN DEBT

The next year slipped by, simply idyllic. With her new partner, Sean, by her side, Lucinda felt almost as invincible as she'd felt travelling the world with strong-man Gregg, who could have told her pigs could fly, and she would've believed him. Sean was more of a serious type, but he believed in her talent none the less, and sparks flew between them as they'd done with Mike way back in the early days, when he'd opened the lid on her world like some jewellery box that had been locked half her life.

He dabbled in photography, and had his own business, which he ran on a bit of a shoestring. It didn't take Lucinda too long to notice that Sean's main quirk was that he was tight with money. If they went out to the pub, she nearly always pulled her purse out of her pocket first. He'd gesture like he was rattling around in his tight pockets for his wallet, but could never quite seem to prise it out. He over-diluted drinks, cut cheese as if he'd been shaving, and only ever ran a bath once a week, using the off-peak heating.

That aside, he was a true gentleman, who'd made it his mission to look after Lucinda. He'd carry her shopping bags, put a footstool under her feet, and always comment she looked beautiful, even when she emerged, hair straggly and dressed in her scruffiest jumper. He'd make her toast in the morning, then would chase her upstairs to her study, where she sat writing. He'd only call when he'd made tea and finally supper. There were no intrusions, no dead-end jobs, just her mind and her computer, plus the calming view of hilly countryside that drifted for miles. The combination was certainly paying off, as she polished off the chapters with the days rolling by. They never spoke about the content in detail, but Sean would give her pointers if she asked, and was always ready to fill in the factual pieces needed, which he'd happily research at their local library.

For a time, it really seemed the perfect match. He'd photograph weddings, and that money would fund not only Lucinda's writing, but also his meagre existence downstairs, in the wing of her house now functioning as a dark room for developing his photos. At times she'd go in there for the peace and quiet and would be fascinated watching the shots develop through the blood-coloured chemical that brought them back to life.

She was more fascinated by the rejected cuttings, which patterned the floor like a who's who jigsaw of family mugshots. Then he explained what he'd do if certain members of the family were spoiling the photograph for the bride's album. He'd never place the "ugly women," as he so brutally put it, anywhere near the centre, rubbing shoulders with her, and those with offensive hats would be asked to move to either side of the photo. He'd save a couple for the hat brigade, but at least for the bride and groom they were archived forever and ever, amen! Serious or not, he had his own quirky ways. He always told the truth, and was brutally honest, no matter whose feelings got hurt in the process. How he ran his business was a shining example of that.

Lucinda's work was finished early autumn, just as the leaves turned crisply green to orange, then fell softly beneath the feet of the postman that inevitably beat a path to their door, delivering usually the devastating news of yet another publisher's rejection. Sean usually tried to make himself scarce by locking himself away in his dark room, but he could hear the sobbing coming from the floor above, and knew only too well that a tantrum would likely follow. Lucinda simply found it impossible to pour something from her heart onto the paper for the best part of a year, only for someone, some unknown amoeba who lived under a rock in another town, to pick holes in what she'd painstakingly created over time. They certainly didn't hold back in their thought or phrasing; a steady stream of throw-away remarks like 'not entirely something that would interest us now or in the future' would land on her mat on a near daily basis. She'd sulk like a thunderous cloud and wouldn't snap out of it for weeks, during which time they barely touched base other than to offer and exchange food like needy next door neighbours.

The pace of it was relentless and took its toll on them both. Sean took to spending the odd weekend with his brother, who lived in the Lake District. It was the brother's spiritual home, where he'd climb the high mountains, go trekking, or take part in a whole spectrum of outdoor sports. Lucinda would feel doubly rejected as the trips became more frequent. The worst happened when one day he breezed in, looking particularly handsome, only to announce he'd be gone the weekend of her fifty-eighth birthday.

"Oh no you won't. I won't be spending my birthday alone," she spat back adamantly, her fiery eyes tearful.

"This is important for me too, Lucinda," Sean added quietly, stroking his silky black hair which fell perfectly back in place. He dressed scruffily most of the time, but that never mattered, because he had his own style. Lucinda liked to think that he deliberately dressed like his father because, if he ever decided to dress his own age, heads would invariably turn, as they did at family gatherings.

"But why would you want to leave me here on my own?"

"I don't want to leave you, Lucinda, you know? It's just this is a really important climb for Pete. He's been planning it for years. You know it's been an ambition of his since he was a kid to do something like this, and he's got the backing of one or two top-class climbers. I can't let him down. He's my flesh and blood."

"If he's your flesh and blood, where does that leave me in the rankings?"

"Listen, Lucinda, if you'd only stop and listen."

"No, you listen, Sean, if you go, we're finished."

His eyes narrowed, face turning ghostly. "You can't mean that, surely?"

"Oh, yes I do, so you'd better think about it long and hard."

He stormed out to the garden, but she could see his troubled reflection on the step beyond the glass patio doors, where he spent an hour, head bowed, slender frame a quiver, shiny black hair masking whatever was going on inside that head of his.

He eventually caved in and apologised, vowing he'd rather share her precious birthday. The whole event sounded the clearest alarm bell yet that there was trouble on the horizon. Lucinda decided to bury her head in her work, doubling her sessions in her study upstairs and hammering the keys of her keyboard, noon and night, like some demented concert pianist. When she announced she was finally finished, Sean suggested she should get away for a holiday, which seemed pretty sensible at the time.

Lucinda wasted no time contacting Ellery, and they unanimously decided that Venice was the place to go. Riding the wave of excitement, they arranged to meet in the city to book it with a travel agency.

On the morning Lucinda was due to go, she spotted a letter sitting benignly on her doormat, and for once she hadn't heard the postman slip it through her door.

"What's this?"

She began reading it as she pulled it out of the envelope. It was a letter from her bank. Just a few short lines to tell her they were suspending her card forthwith, and drastically reducing her credit limit. What it meant slowly started to dawn on her. She had been running up credit on the strength that her manuscript would sell, and if that didn't, her house surely would.

Being faced with the horrible truth, she was thoroughly ashamed of her selfish behaviour and who she was about to let down, as it wasn't her own money she had been gambling with, but her parents' hard earned cash, and they'd worked hard all their lives to ensure Lucinda had a bright and secure future.

CHAPTER NINE

PART TWO:

NEVER ARRIVE PENNILESS IN VENICE
OR IT WILL SWALLOW YOU WHOLE

On the plane journey over from Manchester, everything seemed on track for the pair embarking on their dream holiday. From the clear blue skies, to the clink of champagne glasses, they were on a high fuelled with bubbles and at altitude.

"I've dreamed of sitting in Saint Mark's Square," cooed Ellery, who appeared to be in a dreamy state thanks to the booze, considering she hated flying. So elated were the pair they fell fast asleep, and only woke when their plane was descending.

Ellery suddenly sat bolt upright. "Hey wait. We're going down. I haven't even done any duty-free shopping."

Her tortured expression made Lucinda laugh out loud. "I know, and after you deciding to buy one of those Gucci watches."

Despite the flight attendants buckling up for landing, Ellery's overhead light snapped on, and she was summoning the trolley.

"What about you. Don't you want to buy anything?"

"No, not especially," Lucinda answered, beginning a cover-up that would play out over the next week, until she was cruelly outed.

Their first sightings of Venice blew away any of those doubts: the sparkling canals glistening and inviting; the chants of the gondoliers, in smart navy and white striped tunics; and the higgledy-piggledy buildings that rose out of the water, defying gravity and all sense of time. Their hotel was the Palazzo Giovanelli, in an area known as San Stae in the historic centre of Santa Croce.

Ellery handed Lucinda a hot drink, and that's all she remembered for the next twenty-four hours. When she did rouse, the room was dark, but she could clearly hear running water. How strange, she mused rolling over onto her side. Ellery must be running a bath in the middle of the night. When she woke again some hours later, Ellery was looming large.

"Well, are you going to get up today or not? Don't you want to see Venice?"

Her tone held more than a hint of sarcasm, so Lucinda knew it was time to drag her poor battered body out of her comfortable bed to join the surge of tourists, flowing like the oily water swirling intriguingly beneath them.

"What time did you get up? It was still dark the first time I woke."

"Oh, that was hours ago. I've been out, and explored this whole area while you slept. I've put money on the Italian lottery, and seen some fantastic sights. Are you okay, Lucinda?"

"Yeah, sure. I'm just a little hungover and haven't been sleeping too well."

Lucinda had hinted that she'd have to stick to a tight budget but hadn't fully explained the seriousness of her debt. She had next to nothing to spend, and they were really going to struggle once her cash ran out, as her card had been suspended by her bank the day before they left.

Ellery laughed right back at her, strangely. "Are you sure we shouldn't have gone for a long weekend to Blackpool instead?"

"Ha-ha, very funny. Let's go."

Ellery had spent weeks doing her research, so they wouldn't miss out on her hit-list. They'd have tea in Harry's bar with the pigeons in Saint Mark's square and visit the islands of Murano and Burano. With vaporetto passes that would last them the week, they could come and go as they pleased. The passes also allowed them free entry into certain venues, like galleries and historic buildings.

Lucinda had already researched the cheapest places to eat, where the locals swarmed around little-known bars off the tourist route that specialised in cicchetti.

"What's cicchetti?" Ellery asked, as they marched to the beat of their tourist maps, like film stars with the constant click of cameras teetering on selfie sticks. Couples paused on bridges for the romantic shots, while others were greedily snapping back at buildings from the water.

Without really knowing where they were, Saint Mark's square rose majestically before them.

"Wow!" Lucinda gasped. "It's everything and more. Look at the crowds, and the orchestra setting up in front of that café."

"Let's go find Harry's bar!" Ellery begged, tugging her arm. "I can't wait to eat in there."

"Oh, what's the time? Are you hungry already? I'm still full up from breakfast. Why don't we sit and listen to that stringed orchestra instead. We can have an ice cream or coffee and soak up this amazing atmosphere."

"OK. Then let's do that."

They pushed through crowds of tourists and finally sat down, as the orchestra began tuning their instruments. It was all very formal and grand, with the musicians dressed in white tails with flowery buttonholes, all laid on for their personal pleasure. Lucinda was buying into the fairytale, such was the grand illusion. That was until the menu arrived, and she slapped it flat face down.

"What's wrong Lucinda. Have you been stung?"

"In a way, I have. Quick, grab your bag we're leaving." She almost dragged her friend away in her hurry to avoid the smiling waiter making a beeline for their table. "That is downright robbery," Lucinda gasped, running out of air and choking.

"What is?" Ellery blinked back in her confusion.

"It is fourteen euros to sit at the table without ordering food or drinks!"

"Yes, point taken, but it's one of the world's finest heritage sights, and for good reason. Look around you! Three-sixty views, dotted with iconic buildings you only ever see on postcards. That brick needle is so beautiful," Ellery gushed, pausing her commentary, as though she couldn't quite believe the riches she was seeing as they gazed upwards, pigeons scattering amongst the seated crowds.

"I'd personally love to wander through Saint Mark's Basilica," Lucinda quietly piped up, half the square suddenly draped in shadow.

"Not for me, but you go ahead," Ellery laughed, gesturing towards the end of a mile-long snaking queue full of tourists, tying up their hair and covering bare shoulders. "I'm not much interested in mouldy cathedrals, not when you can soak up this atmosphere."

"Go ahead. Soak it up, at a price! The Basilica costs nothing." Lucinda threw her jacket casually over one shoulder and began strolling in the opposite direction.

"Look, let's eat lunch. I really need to sit down." Ellery was sounding tetchy. Her husband William had given Lucinda a few handy pointers how to keep her travelling companion happy at all costs. It was as if they hadn't known each other from the age of five – now he was suddenly explaining her character.

"Ellery doesn't do small talk, and never ever let her get hungry!"

Despite this, Lucinda was searching for her pocket tour guide, as she'd already circled the cheapest cafes. Of course, they were away from the beauty spots and bustling canals, and judging by her friend's increasing agitation, they weren't about to make it much further.

At the sign of the first eatery, Ellery plonked herself down on a chair, right beside the water with a view of one of Venice's iconic bridges, known as the 'Rialto.'

"This will do me, let's look at the menu." Ellery was already feasting just by putting glasses on. "I'll have a steak, and a bottle of red wine."

"Erm, I'll have pasta puttanesca, and a glass of tap water."

"Wow. Is that all you're wanting?"

"It's more a case of affording."

"Are things really that bad, Lucinda?" Ellery seemed to be mellowing, especially as her glass of red hit home, and was immediately being topped up by a handsome waiter. She smiled and began sawing into her steak with vigour. "Do you want to talk about it? I could always lend you some money until we get back to the U. K."

"No thanks. I couldn't pay you back. You see, I'm more or less less bankrupt. I got a letter from the bank explaining they were freezing my account. My card's already been suspended."

Ellery burst out laughing quite inappropriately and wiped her purple lips by way of apology. "I'm sorry, but you should have told me sooner. We could have sorted something out before we travelled." She emptied Lucinda's glass of water and filled it with wine. "My treat this time. No arguments. I had no idea things were that bad! I don't want you feeling uncomfortable every time we go out. Venice is one of the most expensive cities in the world. No offence, but especially when you're down and out."

"Tell me about it!" The pair giggled, and for once Lucinda's tension lifted. She sank back in her chair and leaned back, immersed in canal life and the clouds whizzing past in Ellery's kaleidoscopic glasses.

Their happy bubble didn't last long, as they were shooed away by the restaurant manager, eager to rake in more cash, the minute they'd scraped their plates clean.

"There is a queue waiting for this table, and you're blocking out a very famous landmark."

"Excuse us for breathing."

Their chairs scraped and they were off, once again pounding the cobbled walkways without ever spotting a place to sit down.

"I think I've got a blister on my heel," Lucinda moaned, stopping to rub her bare feet. Ellery was in no mood for sympathy. With money burning a hole in her pocket, and a friend who was stone broke, they clearly had to come to some new arrangement, and luckily Lucinda's tour guide led them to the perfect spot.

Castello offered some breathing space around the cool Biennale pavilions and public gardens, with its lush botanical pathways, and wooden benches where the pair could finally sit down without dishing out more cash. Ellery looked drowsy. Perhaps it was the bottle of wine which she'd quickly devoured, or the whole crazy situation taking its toll.

After a few minutes silence, she sat up, wide-eyed. "That's it. I've got it. I'll work to your budget."

"What budget? I haven't got one!"

"Exactly!" They burst out laughing.

It was a revelation on such a sunny day, and their outburst sent a swarm of doves into the air like an explosion.

"Okay Lucinda, show me the Venice you've spent weeks researching. Let's make the most of being here without spending a fortune."

Lucinda soon swung into action, and over the next few days, they spent a luxurious day out at the lido sitting on the beach for next to nothing, as they'd waited till after two o'clock when deck chair rates dropped below two Euros, and with the surprising hum of cars in the background. Then it was off to the islands of Murano and Burano, and finally Torcello, an outpost once frequented by Ernest Hemingway.

Ellery seemed to be enjoying the alternative to the bejewelled, Bond-themed experience she'd had in mind, but she was starving, and clearly meagre rations of pasta wouldn't suffice any more. William had warned her about getting Ellery hungry, and on day four, that hanger reared its ugly head in the strangest of circumstances, when they tried to travel back to their new and cheaper hotel in the residential town of Mestre.

The ticket offices were all boarded up, as were the Vaporetto stops. The whole place quickly became a ghost town without explanation, until a young student happened by who could speak pretty good English.

Lucinda was in charge, as her friend was a quivering angry wreck over missed opportunities and hunger. Hunched, pale and sweaty, she'd pretty much dropped out of communication an hour before.

"Excuse me, but where are all the crowds, and water taxis?"

"Oh, they're taking strike action over wages."

"Ah, it's just we're trying to catch a vaporetto and bus back to our hotel in Mestre."

"Excuse me?" The leggy blonde in blazer bent, giggling shyly. She was about six feet tall, in heels, school mini-skirt and tights.

"My English not good?"

"No, it's perfect!"

"No more travelling on the canals today. You must wait here in this car park, for a bus to take us all home. This is the last bus today out of Venice. There's nobody else but us."

"When will the bus come?" Lucinda had a thousand other questions, but clearly the blonde had had enough, and moved moodily away to stand alone in the opposite quadrant.

"What did she say?" whined Ellery. "You're not going to believe her, are you?"

"Who else am I supposed to believe, the invisible man?"

"Hey, no need to get sarky with me."

"Look, let's calm down. This is going to take a while. Why don't you go and grab yourself a bite to eat and get a bottle of wine. I'm not hungry, and am quite happy to keep our places here."

Silence, but she took off nevertheless, like an angry, directionless wasp, and was soon spotted, the same agitated mess, on top of a cliff behind the car park.

Lucinda sank to her knees and sat cross-legged on the red-hot concrete, prepared to calmly sit it out at all costs. An hour passed, still no sign of anyone else. Then, just as the heat cranked up a couple of notches, Ellery appeared at her side, licking an ice-cream. She was like a different person. A young, happy woman in full bloom, thanks to the plonk and half a roast chicken she'd downed while Lucinda had patiently sat it out.

"Here, want some wine? Take some."

"No thanks, I want to keep my wits about me."

"OK, fine, please yourself."

They waited another half an hour, then suddenly a crowd appeared out of nowhere and angrily swarmed till they were surrounded by a scrum of hot, sweaty bodies.

Most of them were teenagers, opening and closing bags for money, and tickets for the one bus that would take them all home. But how? That was what Lucinda wanted to know. She was horribly claustrophobic, and this would really test her willpower: if she'd ever be able to throw herself on and join the noisy throng.

The bus duly revealed itself. It was just an ordinary coach without bells and whistles, and not one of the double buses that she'd seen swanking around, able to turn corners thanks to the rubber accordion band that joined them in the middle.

"Hurry up!" Ellery yelled as she threw herself onboard. Lucinda hesitated a second as the crowd surged forwards, and her feet left the ground as she was scooped onboard. There they hung from hooks, like a couple of chops in a butcher's window, surrounded by the geeky bunch on their mobile phones, trying to get through to their anxious parents.

The bus made agonising twists and turns, whereupon they would each be thrown into the arms of another horrified spotty stranger. The windows were closed, and the whiff of B. O. was nigh on unbearable.

"Don't worry," Ellery called, seeing her friend so anxious and miserable. "You're by the window. Keep looking out for Mestre. We must be getting nearer it now."

The coach pulled into the side of the road, and it beggared belief that the driver was opening the doors to let another muscly mob on. They looked like a gang of labourers returning home for the day, in their hi-vis jackets and hard hats.

It was all too much for Lucinda. She snapped, and suddenly couldn't cope. She had a full-blown panic attack in front of Ellery, who recognised the startling signs she'd never seen before.

"Right. Move. We need to get off. Now!" Her tone worked wonders, and the crowd meekly parted like a scene from the Dead Sea Scrolls.

Once off the bus however, it was a different story, as Ellery soon realised they had a three-hour hike home.

"Never mind your blister. You were the one who wanted off." They marched home in silence.

CHAPTER TEN

NEVER GET DRUNK ON A PLANE

The journey home proved full of surprises, from the long wait at the airport to the ride itself, like no other Lucinda had ever experienced in all her life. Ellery was acting strangely from the moment she woke, which continued as they spent the morning within Venice's Marco Polo airport, with its cooling marble hallways and moving staircases, all designed to get you to where you were going with the minimum fuss and effort, but still with the faint reminder of the glamour you were about to leave behind.

She simply parked herself in one of the downstairs bars drinking red wine as though it was going out of fashion.

"Are you OK, Ellery? You seem very quiet. You will tell me if there's anything wrong?"

"Wrong? Nothing's wrong with me. What about you? You're worse than me when flying."

"I know," she answered sweetly. "I feel okay. I really do, but I'm ready to go back and face reality. Don't get me wrong. I've loved Venice. It's a place I've always dreamed about, and it lived up to my expectations. It's just, I'm ready to face up to the financial mess I've got myself in, and these last few days, I've been missing Sean. He's been my rock, he really has, through the good and the bad."

"That's nice."

Ellery was slumped over the table, slurring her words, though still drawing deeply from her paper cup, which was worrying as they had another three hours before their flight was due to depart.

"How about a coffee, or do you fancy a bite to eat? I know! We haven't bought our duty-free yet."

Lucinda steered her friend around the corner to the duty-free shop, thinking it might be a decoy and offer a little breathing space before her next sip. Her mind was racing and yet she couldn't think straight. They'd got high on the trip out, but that was understandable. It didn't make any sense why Ellery would want to get blind drunk, especially with her husband William meeting them both at the airport.

She had a wild look in her eyes, one Lucinda hadn't seen before, like she was hellbent on a secretive yet self-destructive mission. True to form, she was filling her bags with cigarettes and whiskey, along with miniatures she'd earmarked for the plane ride home. The whole scene made Lucinda feel shaken, with other passengers beginning to stare and point as they swayed along the glossy corridors to gate fifteen.

Finally, their flight was called, as Ellery's eyes had completely glazed over, and she was bouncing off the walls like a pin-ball machine. Lucinda doubted that they'd be allowed to board. Luckily an elderly lady in front needed help getting on the plane with her hand luggage, which allowed just enough time for Lucinda to give Ellery a mighty shove past them and on down the central aisle towards their seats.

"Take your shoes off."

"Why?"

"Because you can't walk in those heels."

"Who said anything about walking? Isn't that the plane's job?"

Despite feeling she wanted to kill her friend at that moment, Lucinda thought Ellery made a very likeable drunk. That is, until she wrestled in her canvas bag and came up for air with another miniature of whiskey and began slugging that as their plane careered to take off.

The passenger in the seat next to them shook his head in disapproval, and asked a stewardess if he could move seats. Ellery was chatting away to the stewardesses, making them laugh, in fact, as they'd chosen to turn a blind eye. It made Lucinda angry when, a few minutes later, another flight attendant brought her another two miniatures of whiskey, adding that he hoped she was having a great holiday.

After blacking out for the best part of an hour, Ellery woke to make a shocking announcement.

"I can tell this is going to be a bad landing. Hey, everyone brace because this plane's going down!"

The lady two rows in front began crying as she bravely finished her crossword, and a baby began to bawl as they hit turbulence.

"See. I told you. We're all going to die."

Lucinda turned her head away and pressed her cheek firmly against the window. She was scared to death, and even more annoyed that her only support was making things worse. She just stared out at the blackness, watching the little fluorescent light blinking on the tip of the wing, a little symbol of hope that they were still in the air.

Finally, they hit the tarmac with a thud, and everybody scuttled off without clapping, leaving Ellery pulling on her latest holiday purchases, the blue high heels that she couldn't walk in.

They made a wobbly descent down the metal staircase, and with just two steps to go, Ellery missed her footing, and did an impressive forward roll onto the tarmac. The ground crew were all laughing and nudging each other, pointing out the pair.

"Take my arm," Lucinda demanded, but instead (and quite unlike her) Ellery slipped her hand in hers, which made them even more unstable, as she was head and shoulders taller.

They were the last passengers to enter the arrivals lounge, and with a lengthy wait to find their cases going around, with passengers three deep in front of the carousel, Ellery leapt onto the moving belt amongst the cases, and it had to be stopped for her safety.

Passengers with onward travel booked hurled abuse at the pair.

"You should be ashamed, travelling in that state."

"Disgraceful."

Finally, they burst through the double doors into the arrivals lounge and facing them was Ellery's husband, holding their coats with an expectant, beaming smile, which soon soured as his wife staggered towards him and ran into his arms crying.

"It's okay. You're with me now."

He glared in Lucinda's direction. She quickly made a break for the toilets, sensing trouble, before the three sat in William's car in silence. Lucinda quickly realised as they sped home, with an atmosphere you could have cut with a knife, that the pair no longer got on. Not only that, but when they did talk, it was making cruel jibes at one another. No wonder Ellery didn't want to return home and had decided to drink herself into oblivion. They obviously both had serious problems to face and said their goodbyes with a hollow hug that said it all.

CHAPTER ELEVEN

NEVER RELY ON OTHERS
TO MAKE YOUR DREAMS COME TRUE

Lucinda returned home to a visible pile of angry looking letters behind her door. Her little cottage looked like it hadn't been lived in since she left, and the return of autumn had forced a drift of dry leaves to pile up outside. Ellery's final words came back to haunt her.

"Make sure you buy a shredder!"

"Why?"

"Because you'll be needing one." She ended with a hollow laugh. "I've been in your position. Take it from me, I know."

Lucinda pushed the door open with her knee and, still in her coat, began dredging through the raft of angry letters solely aimed at her.

She suddenly noticed Sean's spidery writing and ripped the envelope open, trembling. It was like the letter from the bank. She read bullet points, and tears began to splash onto the paper. The gist of it was he'd had enough. Enough of her tears and tantrums. Enough of living like a respectfully quiet lodger. Enough of her and the flat landscape, that always made him hanker for home. It was typical of serious Sean: full of apologies and explanation, but not a hint of hope for their future. So that was that. It was over.

It had been blow after sickening blow, until she spotted a note from her estate agent. "We are pleased to tell you that we have booked a viewing on your property. Please let us know if this is suitable." It was for the next day, but that didn't seem to matter. Lucinda had almost given up hope of the place ever selling. It had been on the market for almost five years, with only a handful of expectant buyers. They were all polite and yet unreservedly together in not wanting to take on what was obviously a 'doer upper.'

She finally removed her coat and began meticulously tidying her house, top to bottom. On autopilot, she began dressing it nicely, a skill she'd improved on over time, then went to bed, calmed by glasses of Amaretto and haunting thoughts of her stay in Venice. Snapshots of life beyond the canals, billowing curtains offering glimpses of opulent splendour, vivid green, red, and gold, and sparkling Murano chandeliers.

The following day Lucinda woke with a headache, though rose and once again meticulously tidied her house. The ritual always settled her nerves before touring with any interested buyer. All she knew was that she waiting for a man called Paul. He owned property in Spain but was returning home because of his ailing elderly mother.

Lucinda preferred showing men around. She couldn't explain why. Maybe women were more fussy about personal style, and hers was undoubtedly quirky and something of an acquired taste.

He gave a quiet knock and greeted her with a smile. He was a small man, around the same age as her, and before she could begin her practised speech, moving endlessly through each room pointing out various features, he spotted her guitar in the corner.

"You play guitar?" He beamed, stating the obvious. "I do as well. Do you mind?"

"No, not at all." Lucinda grimaced. She had never allowed anyone to touch her precious guitar since leaving Mike. It had gathered dust in the corner, but it was too dear to her to throw out, as it represented a happy chapter, freeing her from her dull life, to coming alive with music in her system.

To her astonishment, Paul dropped down on one knee, began strumming and sang directly at her. She noticed his tanned, wrinkly arms, spotted the hands of a true guitarist, and although more than a little embarrassed, complimented him on his voice. This was no ordinary viewing, because they had masses in common. They had both travelled a lot, had a shared love of music, and her practised speech quickly flew out the window as they chatted happily in each room. Occasionally they'd get back to the viewing, when he'd notice this, that or the other.

"Hey, one and a half sinks."

"Yes, that's right, it's very handy."

An hour and a half later they were saying their goodbyes.

"Nice meeting you, Paul. Thanks for coming."

With a foot half out the door, he cheekily added, "I've a whole bunch of other houses to view, but I really like yours, and I'll let you know."

Lucinda flopped down breathlessly on her sofa. She hadn't realised the time, until Paul mentioned he needed shopping before they closed.

A week passed and silence. Lucinda had next to nothing to live on, thanks to what now felt like a prison rather than a home. One day she was driving back up the steep hill to her cottage, when she spotted Paul walking out of her driveway. He didn't recognise her in her car, so she parked and spotted a note slipped through her door.

"Lucinda. Sorry, but the sale of my house in Spain has fallen through. Sadly, it means I can't afford yours. Just was wondering if you'd like to meet up for a drink in the pub? Paul."

Lucinda didn't need this type of distraction. She was not feeling at all sociable, and couldn't afford to go out drinking in pubs. Though not attracted, she was lonely, and did find his proposal intriguing, and so they arranged to meet up that very weekend. Oddly she'd never been to her local in all the time she'd lived there with Sean. He hated the sort of spit and saw-dust hard drinking men's pubs that came alive every Friday and Saturday, nor did he see the point of everyone swapping their hard-earned cash for a crushing hangover.

There she was, standing having this out of body experience with her own conscience in the dimly lit foyer, watching the crowd happily chatting at tables. Paul spotted her and came out to meet her. He had a drink in his hand, and welcomed her warmly, as though they'd never been apart.

"Hey Lucinda. What can I get you?"

"Vodka and lime."

"Ice?"

"Yes, thanks."

They whiled away a good couple of hours, with Lucinda sipping less expensive cola. He was entertaining, quirky, and on paper should have been her type, though still zero attraction.

"Come on. I'll walk you home."

"But it's out of your way!"

"No arguments. I just want to see you home safely."

Paul lit a thin roll-up cigarette, and as they strolled seemed a little out of breath. Lucinda hated smoking. She had inhaled several night clubs in her time and had smoked herself until she began coughing; a similar cough to her father's morning lament, which she didn't want to inherit.

It felt awkward climbing the steep hill at such a slow pace with a couple of street lights out. Paul stopped at the entrance to her driveway, his breath visible and stinking of cigarettes. She was dreading that he'd make a move to kiss her, and it seemed that had been on his mind, but as he bent forwards, a bell sounded in the church nearby, striking midnight, and he pulled away, offering a formal handshake.

"Thank you, Lucinda, for a lovely night." She smiled and watched his figure sway 'til it faded to black.

CHAPTER ELEVEN

PART TWO:

NEVER BE FOOLED BY A STRANGER

Lucinda and Paul met as friends from time to time, only not at weekends, when the pubs were crowded, but during the week, with them both free in the afternoons, when they got the place to themselves, and could chat over games of snooker.

She felt he was holding something back but couldn't quite put her finger on it. He'd be absent from time to time, saying he was flying back to Spain to sort things out, and when he returned, he'd stay with his mother, whom she never got to meet.

This pattern repeated over weeks and months, and she discovered he was drinking too much. He'd ring her every night, and she could hear him pouring his booze into his tumbler, he'd pause, and his speech became slurry. Some of his stories were funny, and some not.

He also threw in the odd, strange fact that caught Lucinda off guard. Like, "I must get in touch with my ex-wife. She's climbing in the Pyrenees now. You shouldn't bear grudges." Or they'd be out walking along the river, and he would suggest the strangest things, like writing a message and putting it in a bottle to float downstream.

"Why would you want to do that, Paul?"

"Oh, you never know where it'll end up or who will find it."

They were meeting up less and less to talk on the phone, though Lucinda now found it strange why she was never invited back to his house to meet his mother. What skeletons might be locked away in his cupboard?

Over time, she found his drunken alter ego far harder to swallow. She'd spend hours listening to him unravel at the expense of her own life. His boasts steadily became more bizarre. His out of the blue statements shook her sideways.

One night, still relatively sober, he asked if she'd join him on a barging holiday with a few close friends.

"Yes, I suppose so. That sounds nice," though the shocking invite seemed to make no sense at all, as he was venturing outdoors less and less, and becoming something of a reclusive liability.

Lucinda decided to stop taking his calls. She knew he relied on her to function, and did feel bad, but thought it might sober him up and ultimately be for the best. A week passed, and she had relished the silence from his relentlessly rambling calls. They'd started to feel slightly threatening, when she'd crack a joke, and he'd get angry.

"Hey, I'm the one that tells the jokes in this relationship. Just you remember that."

Seemingly as a reward, she had found a little spare cash that she'd found hidden upstairs and had decided to treat herself to a steak come Friday night. It felt powerful to have broken free from the clutches of demented Paul. The aroma of fried onions filled the house, but when she moved past her kitchen window to sit and eat her meal she noticed a police van pull up outside.

"Mm, someone must be in trouble," she sniffed, and sat back down. Soon, there was a loud knock at her door, so startling in the unenviable silence she had become used to that she froze and wouldn't answer it.

"That's Paul."

Lucinda ran upstairs two at a time and hid in her bedroom behind the curtains. The knocking nearly drove her mad, and she was waiting for him to break the front door down. She'd have to shout to him and make him see reason. He wouldn't leave and she had no other choice now, scared and at her wits end.

Moving back downstairs, she noticed a long pole sticking through her cat flap.

"Open up, Police!" came the shout that she couldn't ignore. Lucinda opened the door nervously.

"Lucinda Grey?"

"Yes, that's correct."

"A Mister Paul Munroe has reported you missing."

"Really? I've stopped taking his calls, but only because he's being drinking so heavily, and I was being pestered by him on a nightly basis. He came to view my house, and we became casual friends. I'm fine, I just don't want to have any more to do with him."

"He wants us to return something of yours." Lucinda spotted his battered old guitar, and the sight of it brought shivers. She took it, too afraid to get into the significance of what it meant for them both, and watched the police car pull away, leaving a dusty shower settling on her driveway.

Days later when she was walking through town, she suddenly stopped at the newsagent's window. Her eyes were somehow drawn to the obituaries column. That's when her heart stopped.

"Marie Munroe is sad to announce the death of her only son Paul." Funeral service details were followed by "No flowers please, all donations to be paid to Macmillan Cancer Trust."

She read it several times before she could walk and function again.

CHAPTER TWELVE

NEVER LET YOUR HEART RULE YOUR HEAD

Lucinda was becoming used to functioning alone, thanks to repeated misfortunes, but the thought never dawned that the loneliness would last forever, or that her future had already been decided.

One morning sitting in her study, cradling a steaming hot mug of coffee, she glanced sideways at her mobile, which had pinged shrilly against the silence. It was a moment's breathing space for Lucinda, seconds away from her struggle to finish her latest novel. She was more determined than ever to find success. She had the motivation to prove her family wrong, and to put an end to their sniping comments such as "When is this travelling going to stop?" and "Whenever are you going to face up to your responsibilities?"

She didn't recognise who the text was from, and annoyingly it looked like a code. Another puzzle to be deciphered. It seemed slightly threatening, from whoever had sent it, but it only gradually dawned that the shockingly short statement had come from her cousin.

"Mother died some months ago. I'm in hospital. It's not looking good. Get in touch A. S. A. P."

Lucinda pushed her computer away. The news was doubly shocking. They hadn't had any contact for years. Lucinda felt she needed to draw a line under their behaviour towards her. If they couldn't accept her for who she really was, they had no business making a judgement. Their cruel jibes really knocked Lucinda. Over time, it left her badly scarred. They were the only family she had left. How could they have been so cruel? Now this. She couldn't even process how she should be reacting. Sad of course, learning of the death of her aunt, her mother's elder sister, but still slightly bitter at how she'd cast her out when she refused to conform and return from her travels.

Their lives were a million miles from hers. She'd lived her life to the fullest, while they'd played their days out without gambling. Without ever dipping a toe in the water. Without ever being curious to explore the planet they lived on before they died. It seemed such a terrible human tragedy.

Now her cousin was reaching out for help in a real moment of crisis, yet she didn't feel like picking up the thread. She had never helped Lucinda in times of need. Why should she bother?

Lucinda decided to ask Ellery for advice. It needed an outsider's opinion, so she rang her later that night, after pouring herself a large glass of wine, and they soon got down to business.

"I've heard from my cousin. She's got bowel cancer, and she's more or less instructed me that I should be immediately rushing to see her in hospital. I still feel really hurt by the way I've been treated. Blood is thicker than water and all that, but what do you think I should do?"

"I wouldn't go rushing up. It's probably not as bad as she's making out. I mean my father's had bowel cancer as you know, and it's one of the most treatable. You have miles of large and small bowel. They can remove the diseased section and follow it up with chemo."

"Mm." Lucinda buried her head in her glass and took a moment enjoying the strawberry flavour.

"I'm not saying you shouldn't see her, but she's got to learn that you have your own life, and that she can't have you running to her every time she has a crisis."

"You're right, Ellery, as always! Thanks. I'll be in touch soon."

It had been exactly the answer Lucinda wanted to hear. She would go and see her after she'd recovered, but it seemed a tough, yet fair lesson for her to learn. Maybe it would bring them together. She was fond of her only cousin, but they had absolutely nothing in common. She'd chosen to take her parents' path, and had played it to perfection. Becoming a primary school teacher gave her a superior air over Lucinda, and she always made out as if teaching five-year-olds made her more intelligent.

Several weeks later she heard the postman's footsteps coming down her path at speed, scattering gravel. Not another publishers reject she hoped, as a white letter dropped benignly onto her mat. Lucinda picked it up and began reading, but she couldn't make sense of the plain message, delivered like the slap she'd been deserving. It was from a solicitor, informing Lucinda she had an inheritance coming after the death of her only cousin. The unstated sum would be sent by cheque. There were details of where she had been buried. So, her last living relative was now a serial number, on a large patch of Glaswegian grass. They had kindly included a map of her plot, as the city cemetery was so vast. It would be a hard act to settle this with her conscience in the weeks and months that followed.

In the same earth-shattering week, she had an offer on her cottage. The place she'd been so desperate to leave, given her wealth being tied up in bricks and mortar.

With no idea what she would inherit, Lucinda was pretty sure it would be a large sum, as her cousin's moral values had seen her save all her hard-earned cash since leaving school for a rich retirement. There was surely a big life lesson to be learned from her actions.

Lucinda wrote Ellery a letter, with bitter-sweet notes, of a misplaced trust in her judgement, along with a bruised conscience. Ellery was soon in touch, sounding sheepish.

"I feel terrible. I had no idea she was that bad. I genuinely thought she'd get treated and all would be well. I bet it's a bitter pill to swallow." Ellery had a way of cutting through the red tape and hitting a raw nerve when it came to her friend's emotions. "Why don't you come back to the village for a visit? It's lonely for me too at times you know? Even though I belong to a big family and have my brother and sisters living close by. I really miss your company at times. At least say you'll think about it."

CHAPTER THIRTEEN

NEVER RETURN HOME A STRANGER

Lucinda was harbouring a secret on the long drive back to the village she'd grown up in. She was bursting with excitement to share her news, and yet the closer she got to home, with the scenery growing familiar, she felt the same confusing mix of emotions she'd experienced in her youth.

The truth hit home that she was returning a different person, and to make matters worse, she paused outside her old family home, and it was unrecognisable. The new owners had covered the beautiful exterior stone, which had given it its quaint character, with a bolder scheme of plain white render edged in black. There was a glass conservatory on the side of the house, which had made the garden shrink in half. Even their iconic red gate, which had been given many coats over the years, had suffered a damaging transformation and was now a complete colour clash in gaudy purple.

Silent tears spilled down Lucinda's cheeks. It was no longer her family home, filled with a stranger's energy. Worse still, it appeared hostile, broody and forever lost. She wiped her tears and drove on up to Ellery's house. Her mood instantly lifted when she spotted her friend waving madly from her window.

"Hi, you made it! Come on in, I'll make us tea. How does it feel being back in the village?"

"Nice. I enjoyed the drive," Lucinda lied. It was like the two old friends had never been apart, and that was comforting, as they chatted elbow to elbow sipping their steaming brew on high stools at the breakfast bar.

Lucinda kept quiet about stopping off at her parent's house. She needed a moment to recover. They were busily chatting about this person and that, when Lucinda learned the impact of her travels.

"I was out shopping some time ago. Just standing in the queue minding my business, when I overheard this pair discussing your travels through Russia. Of course, my ears pricked up."

"What about my travels through Russia?"

"There was a rumour going around the village at the time that you were drug smuggling!"

"What?" Ellery gave her trademark low giggle at Lucinda's tortured expression.

"I wonder how on earth that started?"

"I'm pretty sure Eddie the postman had something to do with spreading gossip, since he delivered that Red Cross letter to your father."

"Then that was some misrepresentation of the few short lines I sent to my Dad, saying that I was well and happy."

"Surely you're not bothered? You never bothered about your reputation when you were growing up." Ellery truthfully countered.

"That's true. I think we both know that I was no angel at the time, but drug smuggling? That's slander. What other rumours have been spread about me?" Lucinda sighed, raising her eyebrows.

"I shouldn't have told you."

"No, I'm glad that you did. I'm just horrified that it could've been my mother that overheard that."

"If your mother had been alive, you wouldn't have been allowed to be in Russia!" They laughed uncontrollably, and it somehow broke the ice, though the truth had left Lucinda badly shaken by her tarnished reputation within the strict confines of the religious community she'd grown up in. She imagined her mother would be spinning in her grave just miles from where they were sitting.

"Fancy going out a walk?" asked Ellery, jumping down, while somehow threading a chocolate biscuit through the arm of her jacket. It felt good being back with someone Lucinda had known all her life. Ellery was now her closest connection on earth, and obviously their families went way back. She was no longer alone or lonely, but strangely began to worry who she might bump into the minute they stepped outside.

"So are there any of your old neighbours still living around here now?" she asked, sounding deliberately casual.

"Only Pat. Your mother's old next-door neighbour, though now in her nineties, she rarely goes out. She's got Parkinson's."

"That's sad."

"We could pop along and see her later. I told her you were coming to visit." Ellery, a compulsive fast walker, was soon in her stride, leaving Lucinda breathless and struggling to keep up.

The high road in the village had far reaching panoramic views of the river Clyde, where all manner of ships were launched to sail between Gourock, Dunoon and the Isle of Arran. Lucinda had forgotten how spectacular it was. In those days they didn't appreciate views or scenery, they were far too busy tearing around to notice the black navy subs slipping silently through the narrows, leaving a silver slug trail of a wash for miles. You could walk the length of the high road and never bump into another soul, but of course that day as the two old friends were striding out, they bumped into one of the boys from their primary school.

"Hi!" Ellery shouted.

He made an awkward attempt at a smile, though looked as if he'd seen a ghost, turned and watched them till were right out of sight and over the brow of the next hill. His reaction made Lucinda feel even more awkward and out of sorts, rather than feeling at home in her own skin, but for Ellery's sake she played the whole incident down.

Lucinda chose a particularly beautiful spot to stop in at on the side of the road.

"I've something to tell you."

"Right. What is that?"

"I've found a publisher. Can you believe it? It's happened at last!"

"That's brilliant news Lucinda. I'm really pleased. You deserve it."

The friends instinctively hugged, with low clouds rolling past. A great tractor rolled unsteadily towards them, and of course Ellery knew the driver.

"Hi John!" She hollered, stepping in closer to the wall. "How are you doing? Do you remember my friend Lucinda?" He blushed, shaking his head slightly and roared off, leaving them choking on the metallic diesel.

Ellery reached for her inhaler. She once had a bad asthma attack, right about where they were standing, and it had scared Lucinda to death that she might die right there in front of her; yet another powerful flashback to a time and place when she was a totally different person. Now Lucinda felt scared of bumping into her own shadow, as if the old mistakes she'd made in the past had all come back to haunt her. The truth was she was still grieving the loss of her parents and the love of her life Gregg, who'd encouraged her to travel, recognising her talent. Cruelly, she had to cut ties with her remaining family in order to find her voice. Over time, Lucinda was able to accept what had happened, and she'd return more often.

"Hey, wait a minute, Lucinda. You must keep your promise."

"What did I promise? I dread to think."

"You said if you ever got a book published, you would ride through the village naked on a horse! Well, how about it, or have you lost your nerve?" "Me? Never, but I'll let you know when. I don't know why I said that. You know I'm scared of horses, ever since being thrown off that donkey in Southport!"

"Forget the horse," Ellery said, laughing. "I'd be much more worried about anyone seeing me naked!"

THE END

101

EIN HERZ FÜR AUTOREN A HEART FOR AUTHORS À L'ÉCOUTE DES AUTEURS MIA KAPΔIA ΓIA ΣYΓ
ΓEIΣ FÖR FÖRFATTARE UN CORAZÓN POR LOS AUTORES YAZARLARIMIZA GÖNÜL VERELIM S
HJÄRTE PER AUTORI ET HJERTE FOR FORFATTERE EEN HART VOOR SCHRIJVERS TEMOS OS AU'
ΟÏNKÉRT SERCE DLA AUTORÓW EIN HERZ FÜR AUTOREN A HEART FOR AUTHORS À L'ÉCC
ΚΑΡΔΙΑ BCEЙ ДУШОЙ К АВТОРАМ ETT HJÄRTA FÖR FÖRFATTARE À LA ESCUCHA DE LOS AUT
ΚΑΡΔΙΑ ΓIA ΣYΓΓΡΑΦΕΙΣ UN CUORE PER AUTORI ET HJERTE FOR FORFATTERE EE
ΑRIMIZA GÖNÜL VERELIM SERCE ÖÏNKÉRT SERCE DLA AUTORÓW EIN HERZ FÜ
SCHRIJVERS TEMOS OS AUTO AÇÃO BCEЙ ДУШОЙ К АВТОРАМ ETT HJÄRTA FÜ

The author

Carol McAllister was born in Helensburgh, Ar-
gyllshire, and grew up in the seventies, part of a
musical family. A self-taught guitarist, she joined
her father's band as a teenager and continued to
work as a musician for the next fifteen years. Carol
developed a love of food, travelling extensively
through Eastern Europe, Russia and Central Asia,
and kept a diary which sparked her love of writing,
which remains with her to this day.
She is now happily settled in Dalbeattie, Dum-
fries & Galloway, Scotland.

'If you enjoyed this book, I'd be grateful if you'd leave a review on amazon.co.u

Thank you

Carol

ㄴ

Printed in Great Britain
by Amazon

57020472R00061